Overexposed

Ginnie Bond

LIBRIS

An *X Libris* Book

First published by X Libris in 1998
Reprinted in 2001

Copyright © Ginnie Bond 1998

A CIP catalogue record for this book
is available from the British Library.

ISBN 0 7515 2312 7

Photoset in North Wales by
Derek Doyle & Associates, Mold, Flintshire
Printed and bound in Great Britain by
Clays Ltd, St Ives plc

X Libris
A Division of
Little, Brown and Company (UK)
Brettenham House
Lancaster Place
London WC2E 7EN

www.xratedbooks.co.uk

Overexposed

Chapter One

JODI TOOK A long, deep breath as she focused her camera on the naked man. She zoomed in tighter as he worked out by the forest pool, his body glistening with little beads of water from his swim.

The yellow light of an impending storm made him glow, while behind him, dark fir trees threw his athletic form into sharp relief.

Flicking back her blond hair from her forehead, Jodi zoomed in tighter still, and pressed the trigger, reeling off a sequence of close-up shots. It was not her primary purpose to take pictures, but she could not forego this opportunity.

The subject's abdomen was taut and flat, the definition of his pectorals immaculate. The valley between his breasts led her eyes inexorably down. She swallowed hard and panned the camera as the lens poked through the fir fronds of her makeshift hide.

The automatic rewind whirred again as he turned his back; the hollows of his buttocks seemed to be sculpted from his golden skin. When he set his legs apart and bent to touch the grass, she whispered, 'Oh my God,' then rattled off a few more frames.

After he had bent and stretched, he turned. The pelt of his pubis looked like copper in the yellow light. As

1

Jodi pulled the image of his penis into the little square of her eyepiece, she could see he was aroused. It was not a full erection, but enough to make the member stand outwards from his thighs, a branch of flesh with the same brown tan as his body. Wherever he had sunbathed, he had worn no clothes.

The inner surfaces of Jodi's thighs began to tremble. Her solar plexus fluttered. Then, as he raised his arms above his head, thrust out his hips and closed his eyes, she snapped again, praying that the film would not run out.

It did.

'Damn,' she swore, and worked frantically to re-load. But when she looked into the viewfinder once again, the image of her quarry was burned out by the sun. It came from behind a storm cloud, straight into the lens. Shading her eyes, she scanned the forest glade, trying to focus against the light. When she located him her heart-beat almost stopped. He must have seen the reflection of the sunlight off the lens, for he was now sprinting across the grass towards her hiding place.

Jodi panicked. She dropped her bag and ran, leaving her precious camera on its tripod.

As if on cue, the storm stopped grumbling and burst, dropping its rain in sheets. Jodi's heart pounded as she sped between the pine trees. Capturing him in her viewfinder had been titillating; being captured by him was something else – something she did not relish. This wasn't what she'd planned.

Low branches swiped her as she stumbled through the forest. One caught her blouse and sent buttons ping-ing off among the ferns.

She found a path and ran more easily but, behind her, crashing steps were plain to her heightened hearing, even above the harshness of her breathing. As the thunderstorm emptied its contents into that one small part of southern England, Jodi's flight was impeded by soaking shorts. Her summer blouse was plastered to her breasts.

The man had the advantage over her. Apart from being athletic, he had no clothes to hamper him as he paced her, weaving skilfully among the trees.

Now she burst into a clearing and looked about. There was no cover but a large oak tree standing in the centre. Her only thought was to hide there and pray he'd run right past.

A backward look caught a fleeting glimpse of flesh among the branches. Jodi crouched between the tree roots, a gasping, rain-soaked ball.

A bolt of lightning split the sky, its crack sounding like a bull-whip lashed about her ears. Instinctively she flinched. Then, pulling strands of flaxen hair out of her eyes, she slowly raised her head.

Another bolt of lightning lit the clearing. The man had stopped, and stood glistening in a torrent flowing from his shoulders. Unabashed, hands on hips, legs splayed widely, he held his head defiantly against the rain. His phallus curved up proudly. Clearly the pursuit of a female through the forest had triggered in him an urge to mate. That was definitely not what Jodi had planned.

Again the lightning flickered. The late afternoon scene was highlighted with the same stark light as that of a photographic flash. For a fraction of a second this formed an overexposed image Jodi would remember all her life.

It took only a few heartbeats for her pursuer to detect her and reach her in long-legged strides. Now he stood above her, just a pace away, his feet planted widely in flattened grass.

3

The lashing rain abated as suddenly as it had started. The storm swept away from the forest glade, and watery sunlight pierced the gloom.

Jodi tried to avoid looking at his erection, but she could not. It erupted just before her as she scanned the panting torso to the dark-brown, shining eyes. She fixed her gaze on his, trying to determine when he would make his move on her. The wide mouth broke in a knowing smile as his eyes locked onto hers.

'So what have we here? A frightened rabbit?' The timbre of the voice was deep, the educated accent clear.

Jodi tried to bolt but he blocked her, catching her firmly by the arm and digging in his nails. She cried out with the pain as she tried to shake him off but he was far too strong for her.

'No you don't, young lady,' he crooned. 'Don't even think about it – unless of course you want to give me a lot more fun. There's nowhere to hide here, and I'll catch you wherever you run to.'

Jodi froze like an animal caught in the light of a poacher's torch as he glared at her. 'Keep away from me, Dean Bentonne,' she hissed. 'Touch me and you'll feel my knee where it really hurts.' She threw her head back haughtily and ripped herself away.

He raised one eyebrow, then glanced down at himself, his anger turning to a smirk as he stroked his curved erection. 'But isn't this what you came to photograph?'

She leaned back on the tree trunk, defying him to take action. He might have caught her, but if he thought she was going to be easy, he would have to think again.

'Don't kid yourself, Bentonne. I'm not interested in your display.' Liar, she said to herself. The man was turning her to jelly as he stood there, as horny as any man could be. But she kept her blue eyes glued on his.

4

There was no way she was going to let him stare her out.

His brown eyes showed amusement, which annoyed her. In her experience, men of his class had such a superior attitude toward women. Wasn't that why she'd accepted the assignment in the first place – to take him down a peg or two? Just because the fellow was disgustingly rich and sickeningly handsome did not mean that he was above being brought to account for his corruption.

To Jodi's discomfort, he simply stood and smirked. She had thought he'd be angry, that he would hit her, that he would shout and rant at her for spying on him. But he didn't. He was in a much more threatening condition: silent and waiting, studying her face, her lips, her breasts. His own firm lips were moist as he ran his tongue across them.

He stroked his hardness once again. 'Are you just a voyeur, or do you like to touch?' Throwing his head back, he drank the raindrops dripping from the branches. The sinews of his neck went tight beneath the smooth, brown skin. The muscles of his hairless chest stood proud, his abdomen flat now as he drew deep breaths. It made Jodi's belly quiver, and between her legs her secret lips were hot. One breast was bare. Damn! He had only to look at it to see she was aroused.

She pulled at her blouse to cover up the breast.

Now as he watched her, the fingers of his sunbrowned hands clamped his hips, leading her gaze down yet again. He was magnificent. A Satyr with a phallus that reared up stiffly from its mat of auburn hair. Below it hung the largest testes Jodi could ever recall seeing. She closed her eyes but rued it. Images of herself putting her lips to his pouch came flooding into her mind. She opened her eyes again, only to find him grinning.

5

'I asked you a question, young lady. Are you just a voyeur, or do you like to touch?'

Jodi glowered and snapped, 'I'm not going to touch that, if that's what you're hoping!' She put her hands on her hips and stuck her breasts out against the near-transparent blouse.

Amused by her outburst, Dean's eyes twinkled as he studied her. She was all too aware that her shorts were hugging her so tightly that every contour of her form must have been discernible.

She folded her arms across her breasts. 'Do you mind not gawping?'

He smiled such a devastating smile that it took her off her guard. 'I don't mind not looking at you, provided you stop staring at me.'

'I wasn't "staring" at that.' She nodded to his phallus. 'I can't help seeing it if you thrust it out at me.'

'All right. But if we're going to ogle each other on equal terms, you might at least strip off.' He set his head back and laughed.

She glared. 'Try anything and you'll regret it. I'm expert in karate.'

He nodded approvingly. 'Good. I like a woman with fight in her. And as I have a black belt in ju-jitsu, we could have a lot of fun.'

Jodi's heart sank. She had thrown out the lie about her expertise in martial arts as a deterrent. All it had achieved was to raise his interest more.

As she faced him squarely, pale sunlight broke grey sky. It illuminated the glade behind and highlighted the undulating muscles and his youthful features, making him look every bit as slick as a bronze Adonis in some Greek museum.

Damn! All he had to do was stand there exposing himself to her and her anger was melting by the minute.

She was even beginning to hope that he would take her. He would be so strong, so unstoppable. She could imagine him on top of her, the pressure of his mouth on hers. And as she thought about lying in the soaking grass, she could almost feel the pressure of his shaft between her legs . . .

She stopped herself with a mental slap. My God! She was actually fantasising about the brute, instead of planning an escape. She had yet to recover the camera and get back to base with her report that she'd run him to ground at his secret hideout. No report, no pay. No pay, no eat. What a life. But she loved its freedom, even when it led her into the kind of danger she was faced with now. As a tracker in South Africa, and now as a private investigator in England, she was used to taking risks. The contract for tracking this man down would bring her rich rewards. She had got so much material on Dean Michael Alginon Bentonne Junior, high-flying business tycoon and playboy, that her client would be pleased. The bonus she'd agreed on could keep her in champagne and caviar for months – even though she hated caviar and refused the decadence of champagne.

As Bentonne moved towards her, Jodi froze. This was it, then: she could fight or she could succumb. Her fingers wanted to touch his skin, to feel his muscles rippling beneath its sheen. Her palm wanted to cup his balls and hear him moan as she stroked his penis with her thumb.

She stopped herself again. The man was mesmerising her.

'Don't touch me!' she hissed, and tried to move away again but her legs had gone to jelly.

He seemed to sense the emptiness of her threat and, as he pushed her back against the tree, she let out a little squeak. Now he was so close she could feel his breath upon her mouth, hot from his exertion. It flirted with her lips and then was gone.

He grinned again, silent but intense.

With her blue eyes level with his mouth, Jodi stared into his face, fascinated by the full lips as they pursed. Moist with rainwater, they drew in closer. She panted, half with fear and half from sheer excitement.

Studying her with amusement, he whispered very softly, 'No, I don't think you're just a voyeur. I think you want to touch and to be touched. I think you want to play.'

She shook her head hard, her eyes wide, unable to make any verbal denial. The man was right. She did want to be touched, but his finger pressing under her chin felt like a red hot poker against her clammy skin.

'Perhaps you're here to enact a fantasy then?' he whispered. 'What fantasy do you want me to play out for you?'

'I don't know what you mean.'

He smirked. 'Do you want me to suck you between the legs, or to tie you up and spank you? Or do you prefer fellatio?'

Her expression clearly showed a query since he smirked again and whispered, 'I could lay you over that fallen log and whip you with a fir frond, then put my hand between your legs and frig you with my finger until you come.' He smiled widely as he finished, clearly trying to wind her up.

Jodi gulped, unsure if it was the pressure of his hand against her throat or a spontaneous reaction to his suggestions. Again she shook her head without a word.

Now his lips met hers, as he pressed her head back gently, making sure that her mouth was angled up to his.

The kiss was light. It was cool and sweet, and Jodi

felt her tension melting. But he pulled away, just far enough to break the contact with her lips, and whispered, 'Or perhaps you simply want to fuck?'

Oh, my God. Did she want that? She closed her eyes, unable to confront the question. It had been so long . . .

His lips touched hers again, cutting off the thought. His chest came up against her breasts, making the nipples tingle through her blouse. The tingle ran down through her belly and settled deep between her legs. Her clitoris was throbbing; that had started when he had caught her by the arm. The warmth of her excitement was blending with the cold wetness of her rain-drenched shorts at her crotch. Did she want fucking?

She couldn't just say yes, strip me here and now, you horny brute. Even though that might be what her body wanted, she would not allow him the satisfaction of it. If he thought he was going to have her, she'd make him fight for it.

She shook her head and croaked. 'Get off me, Bentonne, or I'll knee you hard.'

His finger stroked her breast as he pinned her to the tree trunk. His lips curled in an almost imperceptible smile.

'So – if you don't want sex, or even mild chastisement, what else could you be up to? Surely you weren't taking pictures for some sleazy magazine?' His face showed the derision of his tone.

'I wouldn't stoop so low,' she protested. The investigative work she did was a thousand times more ethical than that.

His face went hard. 'If you weren't taking pictures for some paper, you must be a spy. And I'm going to teach you a lesson you won't forget for a long time.' The words were angry but the tone seemed to carry just a hint of humour. Was he toying with her, or was he serious?

Jodi said nothing now. Her mind seemed to have seized up, cutting her excuses and her protests. How could she persuade him that her photos were not for publication? She could not tell him that they were intended simply to be evidence that he was playing around.

The strong hand at her throat brought Jodi's thoughts back to her plight and stopped her from moving. As Dean's other hand slipped inside her blouse, she felt cool air upon her skin, then the warmth of his palm as he weighed her breast. He took a nipple between his thumb and fingers and pulled it gently, tugging her senses into life. It shot trickles of excitement down into her womb and made the muscles of her vagina tighten.

Now was her chance. All she had to do was to bring her knee up sharply. That would cripple him for long enough to let her get away, retrieve the camera and get the hell out of there. Her car was only a mile away along a track. She could be out of the forest and on the road to London before he was able to walk.

Her knee would not obey. He had preempted her, in any case, placing his feet inside both of hers and pushing them apart. Now his shaft was in between her legs, pressing on her mount. One hand cupped her cheek as the other yoked her neck.

She was his captive.

She moved her mount to feel his hardness better. Her throat released an involuntary moan as his lips traversed her cheek and whispered in her ear. It was so soft she could hardly hear the words. 'Yes, Miss Sneak-photographer, I think you *do* want fucking.' He thrust his tongue into her ear and made her turn her head away in token protest.

His hand slid down her spine, making her ripple with excitement. Then, as he pulled her mouth to his, the hand slipped inside the waistband of her shorts. She gasped as she felt the heat on her bottom, his middle finger delving deep between her buttocks.

She took his lips by storm, but he withdrew after a few seconds and set a line of nibbles down to her shoulder. She cried out with every bite, then his hand in her shorts pushed down, slipping them over her hips.

She closed her legs to aid him, wanting to be bared. She was molten with desire to mate and wriggled herself against his cock. She needed it inside her, to feel it flush and beat. Thank God she'd kept her contraceptive coil after she'd dumped her last unfaithful lover. It was months since she'd felt a man. Was that really why she'd jumped at this assignment? Had it been to get some excitement into her life, even if it was only to look, and not to have?

Despite her fantasies about Dean Bentonne, she had never in her wildest dreams thought that she might actually have him. As she'd tailed him quite discreetly at high-society parties and formal meetings, he had looked so smart in a business suit, so immaculate in a white tuxedo, so debonair in shorts. She'd watched him at squash and tennis, his power and his grace making her stomach tremble. She'd thrilled when he'd spied her quite by chance as he'd left the Ritz Hotel one summer evening, the brown eyes meeting hers to pass a dart of erotic energy. Did he do that to all the women he met? Then, she had shaken herself out of the trance and recalled that she had been hired to follow him and report his movements. She had been told that he was having an affair, and a jealous lover wanted proof. So far, she'd had no luck in finding them together. But now she'd followed him to a little cottage in the woods, she was beginning to be hopeful. It was the sort of place he might meet a woman he didn't want to be seen with in public. All she had needed were a few frames of them together, and she could have slipped away.

That plan was now blown apart. Bentonne had her like putty in his hands, a quivering mass of contradictions. Her hand slipped around his waist, pulling him tighter to herself. She drew a breath and pushed her pelvis out, whispering, 'All right – so fuck me.'

Part of her could not believe she'd said that word. Most of her didn't care. She needed more than ever to experience him. She'd never had a powerful man like him. So she shrugged off her blouse and slipped her shorts right down. Now she was naked too, gloriously and unashamedly bare. The strong sun was heating up her skin, and her body tingled from its contact with the man.

He pulled her to himself, his lips kissing at her neck, his penis thrusting upward, stretching her pubic skin and pulling up the swollen nub of her clitoris. Oh, how she needed him to touch her there!

'How do you want me to fuck you?' he whispered between his little lip-bites.

She gulped. How did she want him to . . . ?

'Hard and strong against this tree?' He grinned as he thrust her back. 'Or gently in the grass?'

Her hand found his thigh and stroked it slowly. Hell, he was getting her so wet with his dirty talk. Her thigh came up around his hip to feel his skin against the hot lips of her vulva. She couldn't stand this titillation for much longer.

He took her mouth again. First the kiss was warming. Then, as it became more urgent, heat coursed from his mouth to hers. She released her breath in one long sigh. As she felt the steamy heat from his nostrils mingle with her expiration, her stomach began to flitter. Her heart-beat pounded. Her pulse drummed in her ears.

He lifted her, his hands around her buttocks, the fingers spread to cup her flesh. As she rose, she curled her legs about his hips, opening herself to him. She felt the cushion of his glans between her secret lips and released a sigh of pleasure. It had been so long since she had been taken with animalistic passion, and had responded, screaming and clawing, with the same. But since she had banished her last boyfriend from her bed, she had purposely starved herself of men, unwilling to be party to their whims. She had become independent and self-assertive, and had delighted in giving them a hard time when they'd come sniffing around. In the past year of celibacy, no man had managed to turn her on. Until she'd met Dean Bentonne.

Now she was craving. She was wriggling herself against the man to make him feel her slickness and her heat. How could any horny male resist such stimulation?

He pressed her to the tree trunk, the rough bark chafing her skin. It seemed to heighten all her senses as he drove himself against her. But still he did not enter her. She knew that he was teasing her, the bastard. He was making her wait, driving her mad with need.

She squirmed, changing her angle so he could drive into her. She gasped as he bit her neck. As his finger plunged into her nether hole she let out a shriek with the pleasure-pain that it gave.

'All right. You win. I want you, you brute,' she gasped.

He bit her neck. 'But are you prepared to confess your sins before I give you what you want?'

Jodi began to sob. The finger in her anus was sending her delirious as pleasure speared through her body, making her nipples harden. Her clitoris stood erect as she rubbed her pubis on the phallus of her captor.

'Don't fool around,' she pleaded. 'You've got me where you want me. Isn't that enough for your damned ego?'

He took her mouth and kissed her slowly. Then he whispered in her ear, 'Tell me the true reason why you're here and who you're working for.'

'It's more than my career's worth to tell you that.'

His tongue began to probe her lips with darting movements until she gave it access. Then he thrust it deep into her mouth. As his tongue-tip met with hers, a thrill shot up the insides of her thighs, and the nub of her clitoris pulsed. But the flirting tongue suddenly withdrew, leaving a sense of disappointment mixed with yearning for its return. Still he held his mouth to hers, riding her lips, sensual but demanding.

'Confess,' he whispered. 'Tell me who you're working for.'

'Go to hell,' she gasped. 'You know I can't.' She gripped his thighs between her knees and rubbed against his phallus. She wriggled to make the tip of it slide between her labia.

Suddenly she captured it. Its heat felt really marvellous as the swollen head rippled up inside her. She cried out, partly with elation but mostly with relief, and sank down on his cock to feel it deeper still. She almost had it all.

Until he pulled it out of her and pushed her back against the tree.

Chapter Two

JODI OPENED HER eyes as Bentonne withdrew his cock, angry and surprised at his unexpected move.

He stood before her proudly, his cock erect, the helmet glistening with her juice, and his hands back on his hips again; his face was lit with triumph. Thrusting his pelvis forward, he threw his head right back, letting out a laugh that echoed through the clearing.

Jodi glowered. He had been toying with her. He had worked her up, then cheated her. Worst of all, he had made her almost plead with him to take her. Her anger welled, feeding off the energy of the unconsumed erotic fire he'd lit.

'Well,' he chuckled, his rich voice rippling his diaphragm. 'I think that makes us even, don't you? It's a pity you haven't got your camera now. I'd like a shot of your expression!'

Fury rose in Jodi as she took a step towards him, hissing, 'You low-down, rotten bastard!' Her foot flashed towards his crotch but he side-stepped the emasculating swing. In the same move he caught her ankle, pulled and twisted it, spinning her off balance.

Jodi screamed as she felt an excruciating pain. In the

next instant she found herself flat on her stomach, her mouth eating grass, her leg pinned back.

'Don't fool with me, young lady,' he growled. 'If you want to play this kind of game, I suggest you take some lessons first.'

She curled her lip and snarled, 'You arrogant pig.' Then she twisted her head around and spat grass at him. 'You've broken my ankle.'

She felt his hands, probing but gentle in their exploration of her foot. She yelped.

He slapped her naked bottom. 'Don't be a baby. It's only a sprain. It'll probably swell a bit but it'll be all right by tomorrow, although it would damned well serve you right if I had broken it.' He let go of her leg. 'Get up. We've got some serious talking to do.'

Petulantly, Jodi got to her knees. When she tried to stand on the ankle she winced with pain. She took a couple of hobbling steps and stopped, desperation running through her. There was no way she was going to be able to escape from him now. Naked and cooling quickly, he had her where he wanted her.

'You won't get anything from me, Bentonne. I'll die before you make me say a thing.'

'Perhaps you will. I don't think you realise what you've got yourself into.' His face had lost that alluring smile, and the light in the brown eyes had died with it.

'Go to hell,' she hissed. But as she made a half-hearted effort to go, he caught her arm. A wry smile passed his lips before his expression became dead-pan.

For a moment, Jodi stared into his face defiantly, and tried to wriggle free. 'You're bruising my arm. I'll scream if you don't let go.'

'Scream, then.' He let go and made a sweep with an open palm around the clearing.

The sunlight that had followed in the wake of the

storm was waning. In the dimness, the surrounding woodscape had become sinister. Jodi shivered. The balmy afternoon was cooling. She must get warm. But her wet clothes lay where she'd sloughed them off, and she had no dry ones in her car.

Bentonne's skin steamed as he eyed her nakedness. 'You'd better come with me.'

'Not on your life,' she snapped.

'All right. But I don't envy you spending the night out here, with wild animals on the prowl.'

Jodi searched the edge of the wood. She half expected to see pairs of slitted, yellow eyes hungrily casing her every move. As a child and adolescent, she had been used to the openness of the South African veldt, but this English forest was so closed in. It was secretive and brooding: anyone or anything could be watching her now without detection. She turned to Bentonne despairingly.

He frowned. 'Look, I'm not prepared to spar with you. Are you coming quietly or am I going to have to drag you?' As he watched her thoughtfully for a couple of seconds, the light came back to his eyes. 'Or is that what you want to complete your fantasy? Do you want to be dragged naked through the woods?'

'You're perverted,' she sneered, trying to stop a ripple of excitement running through her.

Bentonne laughed. 'At least I'm honest. I don't indulge my perversions by hiding in the bushes watching someone bathe.'

Jodi kept her defiant attitude. There was no way she was going to give in to him now. For the time being, he had lost his erection, but she had no doubt that he could get that back at any time. It was clear that he intended to keep playing with her – and probably planned to have her when he was ready.

17

He picked up her clothes and turned. 'Are you coming or not?'

Jodi scowled and took a step forward. Then she creased as the pain in her ankle shot up through her leg.

'Hop on your good leg,' Dean barked with the tone of someone who was accustomed to being instantly obeyed.

Jodi hopped a pace and stopped, unable to keep up the effort.

Bentonne frowned. Then he hoisted her effortlessly. With one arm around her back, the other under her knees, he pulled her tightly to himself.

She did not struggle. But neither did she hold herself against him. There was no way she was going to give him illicit pleasure from his apparently noble act.

As he marched briskly along a pathway, she cried out as branches swiped her bottom and her face. Turning away from them, she found her cheek against his chest, his heart pumping loudly with exertion. Or was it with excecitement? Was he imagining how he was going to have her when he got her to the cottage? But what of his assignation with some woman? Her spirits leapt. Another woman might be an ally against the man. But then Jodi's heart sank again. The woman might enjoy a threesome, or even a lesbian encounter – something Jodi had never had.

'Can't you be more careful?' she snapped as a bare branch scraped her buttock.

He laughed. 'That's mild compared to what you're going to get in a minute.'

Pictures of whips on naked flesh crept into her mind. She almost felt shackles around her wrists, tying her to a bed, almost saw Dean's wide mouth grinning as he forced her legs back brutally and put his mouth between them.

18

She thrust the fantasies away. Damn it, this was serious! It was no time to be thinking things like that.

They passed the tree where Jodi spied her camera on its tripod. It stood sentinel, its single eye staring at the lake. She groaned. Only her blind panic could have made her abandon the most valuable thing she had.

The cottage came into view, its dark thatch bearing weightily on bulging, whitewashed walls. At the side, a shed leaned lazily against it; a jeep from the Second World War stood within, camouflaged by shadows.

A picket gate led to the stone-flagged path. The door latch clacked, and the squeak of hinges announced their arrival. Jodi passed under an oak lintel, then a black-beamed, smoke-browned ceiling. The floor was strewn with matting, and lumpy white walls and gnarled woodwork completed a rustic scene.

Unceremoniously, Bentonne dumped Jodi on a bed. She shook herself into life and sat up, swinging her legs over the edge. There was no way she was going to lie down and open her legs like some willing whore.

Dominating her field of view, Bentonne stood before her, his penis large but flaccid. Despite her resolve not to get excited, Jodi's inner thighs quivered uncontrollably. She clamped her arms across her breasts as he glowered down at her.

'Now – tell me what I want to know, and I might just let you go.' He hooked his finger hard under her chin and made her look up into his eyes.

Jodi heard Bentonne's voice through a daze. She needed time to adjust, needed to collect her strength to fight him off. He pulled one wrist away from her breast and held her pulse, counting like a doctor would. She snatched her arm away as soon as he had finished.

Walking to the outer door, he turned a large iron key and kept it in his fist.

'You can't keep me here,' she snarled. 'That would be kidnapping.'

He shrugged. 'I'll keep you here until I've had what I want from you. We can do it the easy way or the hard way. I don't care which. You got yourself into this, so don't blame me for the consequences. I'll run a bath for you. It'll stop you going hypothermic, and it'll do that ankle good.' With that, he ducked through a low doorway into another room.

Jodi shivered. She sat right on the edge of the bed, feeling damp in body, low in spirits. At the sound of running water she become more apprehensive. There was no way she was going to get into a bath with him or on her own.

The room felt cold. A small window over the bed admitted a miserly amount of light. The last of the summer sun had sunk behind the trees. She kneeled up to the window and tried the catch but it was fixed, so she scanned around to see if there was any other way she could escape.

The room was of modest size, five good paces square. The bed, a simple wooden chest, a table and a fireside rocker were the only furniture. A brick hearth held the embers of a fire, which had left a hint of pine smoke in the air.

Jodi shivered violently. The cold and the mixture of fear and excitement had drained her energy reserves. The way Bentonne had toyed with her had contributed to this depletion. If she did get out alive, she swore that she'd get even with him if it was the last thing she ever did.

A tear tracked slowly down her cheek, and she fiddled with a gold ring on her finger. Whenever she was frightened she did this. Turning it round and round, she wished that it was a magic ring and that it would transport her back to the relative safety of her dismal London flat. Though it was the scene of failed affairs and loneliness, it was preferable to this. Or was it? There had been a core of coldness inside her body for some months. For a few moments, the heat of passion that Bentonne had caused to rage in her had melted that chill away.

She picked up her wet clothes with dismay. The blouse she had chosen in the scorching afternoon had been inappropriate for her clandestine mission. She should have worn khaki like she used to in the veldt. She should have worn slacks to protect her legs; and she should have gone barefoot instead of wearing trainers, but her feet had become so soft from wearing shoes.

Jodi snapped out of the depression. It was time to be thinking of escape, not feeling sorry for herself. She was a prisoner for the moment, but not for very long.

When the door swung back, she stood up quickly, bearing most of her weight on the good foot.

'Your bath water's ready. Want a hand?'

She looked at Bentonne as he stood in the doorway dressed only in denim shorts, his auburn hair groomed smartly, his face looking smug at her annoyance.

'No, I do not want a hand. And I'm not getting in any bath.'

'You'll do as I say. It'll warm you and put some colour into your face. I want you alive, miss.' He smirked, then continued with a wider smile, 'For tonight at least. I've put some herbs in the bath to heal your ankle. I'll rub it later with some liniment. That will take the swelling down.'

'You'll keep your hands off me if you know what's good for you.'

He raised an eyebrow. 'Look – I'm only trying to help. I'm sorry I ricked your ankle.'

Jodi scrutinised her captor. Although there seemed to be genuine concern in his eyes, she didn't trust him. She was sure that he was employing softness to get her guard down. She could sense that he was scheming something. She could also see the tell-tale bulge in his shorts, despite his hands thrust deep into the pockets.

'Don't gawp,' she snapped, looking down at her own nudity. 'And you can stop playing with yourself.' She nodded to his badly camouflaged erection.

'I can't help it if you arouse me. Has anyone ever told you how provocative you are? And how beautiful?'

'Don't think you can get round me with that crap.'

He stiffened, a dart of anger shooting through his eyes. 'Look – I didn't invite you here, so don't complain if I get horny.' Then his smile came back and made him look oh-so boyish. 'And if I want to say you're provocative or beautiful, I will.' As he adjusted himself in his trousers, Jodi thought he looked sheepish. She had found a chink in the self-assurance and decided to widen it. She'd make him feel as uncomfortable as he was making her.

'Are you planning to rape me?' Jodi thought she caught the clear eyes showing just a tinge of hurt.

He smiled wanly. 'Is that another one of your fantasies?'

Jodi ignored the loaded question. 'Are you scared to try?'

Bentonne smiled grimly. 'I'm not scared of you. Not like that, anyway.'

Jodi detected a hint of doubt in his expression. He was scared of something. 'Why are you keeping me here, then?'

This time he smiled more freely. 'Because I intend to find out who you're working for and why you were spying on me. But right now, I'm going to chop some firewood. Why don't you take the opportunity to get yourself warm?'

Again there was a genuine note to his words. Jodi half closed her eyes, as if this would give her an X-ray view of his true intentions.

He pulled the key from his pocket and went towards the door. 'No, I'm not going to rape you. It's not my style. But I am going to keep you here for a while. If you give me what I want, I might let you go. If not – well, let's just say that people have disappeared without trace in this forest. I'll give you some time alone to think about your situation. Don't try to leave. You wouldn't get far.' He left, locking the door from the outside.

Jodi didn't believe that he would not force her if she resisted him. She glanced through the window to see where he had gone. Outside, the storm was brewing once again. She pulled the curtains to, but there was still a gap of brooding greyness where the material didn't meet.

She shivered. His threat to make her disappear was scaring. If she was going to get out alive, she would have to use all her wiles. She might even be wise to acquiesce to his sexual demands. At least that might stop him hurting her physically, and it might even be quite enjoyable. But whatever he did to her, there was no way she could tell him who her client was.

Making up her mind to use the time wisely, Jodi hobbled into the room beyond. The scene was like an illustration in a Victorian picture book. In a quaint kitchen, flickering light came from an oil lamp hanging over an old pine table. A huge black range radiated welcome heat, though the flagstone floor froze her feet. The leaded window reflected the lamplight from the gathering darkness of the storm. It also mirrored her in a dozen diamond-shaped images. Jodi shivered to think

23

that anyone might be out there, viewing her without her knowing. Had Bentonne gone outside to watch her through the window while she bathed? She drew the curtains.

There was a door beside the window which opened to her touch. The disappointment at finding a primitive toilet instead of an open yard was only moderated by her need. She took advantage of it. At least that was not going to be a problem for a while.

At the end of the table sat a crusty cottage loaf, a knife with a block of moulded butter by its side. A thick slice lay on a terracotta plate, its buttered wholemeal texture too inviting to resist. Jodi was ravenous. The sight of the bread and the smell of stew coming from a black iron pot chuntering on the range made her even more so. She had not eaten since an early afternoon picnic before she had left her little car and tracked Bentonne to the cottage.

Tearing at the crust, she scanned a cavernous bath steaming invitingly in a corner, an aroma of herbs on its breath. Sweet scents and woody notes wreathed up to her nostrils. Thick white towels hung softly over a brass rail on the range, and the water beckoned. She had to get warm, if only to survive the night. Tomorrow she would escape.

After another wedge of bread, she hobbled to the bath, grumbling loudly to herself about men.

With two hands on the bath rim she lowered her body, inch by careful inch, until she was immersed up to the neck. As her long hair floated out around her shoulders, she sighed and closed her eyes.

Whatever possessed you to take this crazy job, Jodi Barens? she whispered to herself. You must have been quite mad. But then she recalled that she had accepted the job partly to take the man down a peg. He was arrogant and cocky. It had made her sick to see him when he sported in public with some rich or famous woman on his arm, particularly since he was supposed to be engaged to the Crown Princess of Lechtendorf and Grattenburg – or some such outlandish place. Jodi could not quite remember what her agent had said when he'd offered the assignment. All she had been told was to watch him closely and report in every day. The contract also required her to take a few confirming pictures of him fooling with a woman, but she had got a bit over-enthusiastic when she'd seen him by the lake. Should she keep those pictures for her private album? She cupped her face in wet hands. If she was absolutely truthful, she might. The bastard turned her on. That time when he had smiled at her as he'd left the Ritz had made her fantasise about him every night for a week. But he was the enemy, for god's sake. He was a million-aire playboy. He was everything she disliked about people with power whose families had made their money at the expense of the downtrodden. Christ, she hissed to herself as she sank deeper into the heat. She was thinking like that Marxist pig of a boyfriend she had dumped a year before. 'Damn,' she swore, and closed her eyes.

In a few minutes the heat and the herbal infusion had started to soothe her cares as well as her swollen ankle. After another few minutes of breathing the aromatic mixture, her mood began to change.

She had nearly had Dean Bentonne make love to her. And, although he'd rejected her, he was clearly inter-ested in her sexually. Now, she was sure that if she played him right, he might try it on again. When she had him where she wanted him, he might become less interested in finding out about her assignment and more passionate about herself. That was the only worthwhile card she had to play. When she'd softened his defences, he might let slip who he was seeing in secret.

Jodi's forefinger slipped between her legs. Her labia were still swollen, and her clitoris rose to her touch. As her breasts floated in the scented water, they felt nicely tight. She had forgotten how long it had been since a man had made her feel like this. The way she had reacted to Bentonne under that tree had surprised her. She hadn't realised just how much she'd missed a man's urge to mate and his strength as he pinned her down and forced her legs apart. Of course she'd always let them do it, pretending they were too strong for her to resist. She'd egged them on with coy little looks. But none of her boyfriends had been as raunchy as Dean Bentonne, and certainly none were as rich. She'd wanted to go down on her knees and mouth his cock. My god, what a cock he had! Even thinking about it now made her horny again.

He might be a brute of course; some men were made that way. They seemed not to know how to caress and touch and kiss you where you wanted them to kiss. But if Bentonne was a brute, that was all right because she sometimes needed to be taken so powerfully that she really could not resist.

But what if he was gentle? Somehow that did not fit his character or his build. He was a hunk, not a Romeo. His athletic body would be wasted if he didn't wrestle her as she pretended to fight him off.

'Damn,' she swore again, thrusting the fantasy aside. She was as horny as a doe on heat. What the hell had she got herself into?

Chapter Three

JODI AWOKE FROM a doze as she heard the door latch clack. She sat up abruptly in the bath. How long she'd slept she did not know.

Bentonne looked at her grimly as he entered, his naked torso glistening with sweat, his abdomen pumping as if he'd been exercising.

She glared. 'Do you mind? I'm in the bath.'

His mouth curved slightly. 'I don't mind at all, Miss Barens.'

She sat bolt upright now. 'How do you know my name?'

Emptying the contents of her briefcase on the table, he picked up some papers and sat on the side of the bath looking down on her.

'You bastard,' she hissed. 'So much for going out to chop wood.' He'd found her car at the edge of the estate. Now he had access to all kinds of information in her briefcase. She had been a fool to bring it on such an assignment.

'Jodice Marie Barens,' he read. 'Aged twenty-three years. Anglo–Dutch parentage. Dual nationality. Brought up in South Africa and England. Educated at West—'

She tried to snatch her curriculum vitae from him but he whisked it away. All the time, she was aware of her nudity, her breasts swinging as she lunged towards him.

Bentonne grabbed her hand and held it so she couldn't get the paper as he continued: 'Educated at Westdean Academy for Young Ladies.' He studied her closely, smirking derisively as he said, 'Young ladies?'

'I don't care what you think, Bentonne. Now get out. I want to—'

Flattening his expression, he read on. 'Worked for Greenpeace for a year.' He looked quizzically at her again. 'So – you were one of those wretched environmental protesters, were you?'

'If you're asking if I was an activist against firms like yours which rape the planet and enslave their workers, the answer's yes.'

He shrugged. 'Save me the sermon, Miss Barens – Freelance Private Investigator.'

'You shit,' she hissed, trying in vain to pull her hand away from his grip. She watched anger spark in his eyes. It was gone in a second, but it made her recoil. It gave her another insight into that hard streak running under the good-looking exterior. She remembered his threat that she might disappear if he didn't get what he wanted.

Now she glared back at him as he viewed her unashamedly between the legs. It made her nervous to have him so close. But as his fingers wove between her own, that excitement she had felt in the forest started to course through her once again.

Their roles had been reversed, and he pored over her, intimately, just as she had focused on him through her lens.

He let go of her hand as he turned the pages.

Folding her arms across her breasts, she shut her knees in a gesture of defiant modesty.

He pretended to continue to read. 'A prodigious sexuality. Needs fucking at every opportunity.'

'Chauvinist. What happened to the suave image you show in public?'

That didn't deter him. She could see he was enjoying taunting her. 'Very nice boobs, and a surprisingly large pussy for such an elegant young woman.'

'And crudeness doesn't suit you either, Bentonne,' she snapped as she pulled her heels up to her buttocks. 'You're perverted.'

'Not as perverted as you.' A broad smile spread across his face.

'I am not a pervert.'

He shrugged dismissively as he knelt beside her, his face a few inches from her own. 'Normal young women don't sneak around like you were, sweetheart.' He trailed a finger through the water under her legs, sending little currents against her vulva. She was sure that he knew what he was doing to her. She thrilled as his finger traced the outline of her arm and then her neck. Even so, she tried to push him away, but he caught her fingers again. Momentarily he put them to his lips and kissed them.

'And you can stop that. You won't get round me like that.'

He smiled thinly, whispering, 'I don't need to get "round" you. I can have you in any way I like, as soon as I like and as often as I want you. I'm going to tie you up and take you in my time, very, very slowly. And if you struggle, I'll spank you for the naughty girl you are. But before I do, you're going to tell me who sent you here and for what purpose.'

She threw her head back haughtily. 'No one sent me. I came of my own free will.'

'So you're just a nymph looking for a good time?' He touched her nipple, lifting it so that it stiffened and sprung back as he let it go.

'No, I am not.'

'Not what? Not a nymph, or not looking for a good time?' He laughed. 'When you stripped your knickers off so urgently under the tree, I could have sworn that you murmured, "Fuck me".' He whispered it so that the words sounded almost romantic.

She turned away, the memory sending pulses of energy to her labia. Her face began to burn.

'Ah – so you don't deny it!' He slipped his hand under her buttock and skimmed it through the furrow of her sex.

She clamped her legs and glared, but she was helpless to stop his taunting. Secretly, she was more stimulated than if he'd made love to her tenderly.

She slitted her eyes. 'You seduced me. I don't normally behave like that.'

'That's not what this tells me,' he smirked as he reached for a letter from the table.

Dear Jodi, I need you desperately. I've tried to call you but all I get is your answer phone. Please ring. No other girl I've had is as voracious for it as you are. Let's get together and be animals like we used to. Please.

'Give me that, you pig!' Jodi caught the letter and ripped it, but she only got the part Bentonne had read out. He studied the rest, letting out a long exclamation. Then he looked at her with his eyes alight before reading: *'You're the only girl I know who attacks me when she wants it, and likes to be spanked on her hands and knees while I . . .'*

30

She tried to snatch again, but Bentonne was too quick for her.

'. . . *while I do you from behind*,' he whispered as he read the last sentence. 'Well, well. So, you don't normally behave like a nymph?'

She hid her breasts. It was partly to disguise the fact that her nipples were twice their normal size and the nimbuses were swollen with the excitement of the confrontation. Despite her annoyance at Dean's superior manner, her heart missed a beat every time he showed that devastating smile. She quivered inside as the brown eyes flashed again. He was so much more exciting than her ex, who thought he could get her back by reminding her how much she had enjoyed having him.

She looked him straight in the eyes. 'I suppose you think reading my private papers is very clever. Well, it won't make any difference, so do your worst.'

Bentonne whispered, stroking her nipple again. 'Perhaps I will do my "worst" if you don't give me what I want. You still haven't told me who sent you here to spy on me.'

'I came to get some wildlife shots for a book I'm doing.' She pushed her wet hair back defiantly. 'I happened to see you swimming in the pool and—'

As his lips curved at the edges, her solar plexus fluttered, but she held his eyes stonily.

'You're a lousy liar,' he whispered, pulling her nipple so that it stood up proudly. The sensation sent trickles of energy down into her clitoris. No matter how she clamped her legs, she seemed not to be able to stop it.

She pushed his hand away. 'You can stop that. I want to get out. This water's getting cold.'

He pulled the plug and watched as the water spiralled away. Every inch less made Jodi feel more vulnerable.

'And you can stop leering!' She tried to curl up smaller, using her legs as a barrier to hide behind.

'Why should I? I don't often have the pleasure of having a nymph in my bath.'

Jodi tossed her head back. 'What about your girl-friend?'

'I don't know what you mean.' His face was straight as he said it, and she was almost convinced that he did not know whom she was referring to. For the first time she began to doubt the certainty of her information about Bentonne meeting a woman in secret. There had been no woman's scent, no panties or bra on the floor-boards by the bed.

'Aren't you having a fling with someone?' Jodi looked straight into his eyes, not giving him a second to evade her question.

His face went hard. 'Let's get something straight, shall we, Miss Barens. I wouldn't take any woman anywhere where some sneak like you could spy on us. I'm not that stupid.'

She pushed her hair away from her forehead; her mind raced. Surely her source had not been wrong about Bentonne fooling with a woman? The client had agreed to pay her very well to locate him and get hard information on them both; so Bentonne must be lying.

She went to rise, but he pushed her down. She turned away but he wrenched her face around to meet his.

'Who sent you, Jodi? You might as well tell me volun-tarily. I'll screw it out of you one way or another if you don't. The choice is yours.'

'And I told you – nobody sent me.'

Jodi's pulse was drumming at her temples. She closed her eyes, unable to look at him without betraying the excitement running through her. Danger had always set her alight. When stalking big game on the South

African veldt, the excitement had turned her on, even when she had been young. When a wildebeest had chased her up a tree, she had had an orgasm so wonderfully violent that it had been years before any man had produced one half as pleasing. Now she was getting the same kind of charge from being cornered by Dean Bentonne. She sensed that he was dangerous, but could not stop her excitement at his closeness.

He turned her shoulder roughly. 'I know you're lying, Jodi. There's more to you coming here than you're telling.'

She smirked. 'Yes, I think there is. My source said you spend your weekends screwing in the woods. Do you have any comment for your fiancé?'

He laughed. 'Surely you don't believe that. My so-called engagement is something put about by the press.'

'Is it?'

'Yes, it is. I'm not seeing any woman, so don't think you're going to catch me in compromising situations. His finger stroked her cheek again. 'Now – are you going to be a good girl and tell me the real reason why you're here, or do I have to torture you?'

'You wouldn't dare.' She blanched and bunched up tighter to keep warm, once more acutely conscious of her vulnerability. If there was no other woman at the cottage, her own position was even more precarious than she'd thought.

'All right,' Bentonne grimaced. 'I'd hoped that I wouldn't have to resort to torture, but . . .'

She watched with alarm as he opened the fire door of the range. Thrusting in a brass poker, he threw a wicked look at her.

She eyed the poker fearfully as he turned it in the red-hot coals and checked its heat. Then her nerve cracked.

'Look,' she croaked, 'you don't have to do this. You can screw me all night, all ways, if you want to. You can tie me up and whip me. You can have me over the kitchen table, or hanging from a branch out in the forest, but put that poker away.'

Bentonne turned and grinned wryly. 'More of your fantasies are they, Jodi? You're quite a girl for unfulfilled sexual dreams, aren't you?' He pulled out the poker again, glowing red, and turned it towards her.

She put up a shaking hand. 'All right. I wasn't shooting wildlife. But I was telling the truth about being hired to get pictures of you with some woman. I was told that your fiancé wants proof that you're playing around. But I was sworn to secrecy about that.'

He turned on her, his features hard. 'Surely you don't believe I'd fall for a line like that. And do you really think that any woman with the slightest degree of breeding would come to a place like this for a romp?'

That made her seethe. The man was right, but she would not be put down by his smugness. 'Deny it all you like, Bentonne. My instinct tells me you're covering something up.'

He studied her thoughtfully then smiled. 'What could I possibly hide in a place like this?'

'You could meet someone brought in by helicopter.' She was grabbing at straws and she knew it, but she had to get something good on him soon or she would not get her final payment.

He shrugged. 'Have you heard any helicopters?'

She raised her head proudly even though she felt small.

'So tell me the truth and perhaps I won't torture you.' He moved towards her, the poker glowing.

Jodi leapt out of the bath, but she had forgotten her injured ankle and shrieked as it let her down. She rose and hobbled towards the other room but he was on her in a trice, the poker clattering on the flagstones.

She screamed and tried to fight him off, but he caught her. One hand slipped around her waist, the other between her legs, but her skin was wet and he couldn't get a grip.

She wriggled free and darted towards the outer door before he tackled her on the mat. She lay on her back before a roaring fire, steam rising from her naked body. His knee came up between her legs as she twisted and squirmed under him. But when he bore down, she gave in. He was far too strong for her.

He pinned her arms above her head; her labia slipped on the hardness of his knee. She could feel his erection too, stiff against her thigh, only the material of his shorts preventing her from feeling its supple skin against her own.

'Prick,' she spat, as his face came down to hers. 'I'll see you hang for this. And I'll—'

He bit her neck and made her squeal, but as she turned to bite him back, her lips met his. Pressing his mouth to hers, he quietened her, and as the kiss went on she began to go quite limp. He started to grind her slowly with his knee.

As she widened her legs to feel him better, he let go of one arm and moved his hand to her breast. The nipple stiffened quickly, and when he plucked at it she moaned with the excitement that it brought her.

The kiss went on. It was as if he was not prepared to risk letting her mouth go free. Then, as he moved himself slowly up and down her, she sighed at the feel of his cockshaft rubbing on her groin. Finally he took his mouth from hers and looked into her eyes, stroking her cheek gently with one finger.

'I'm sorry, Jodi,' he whispered,' I would never have

hurt you with that poker. You're far too beautiful.'

'You're a bastard,' she croaked, tears rolling down her face. 'You're a rotten bastard and I hate you.'

'And do you hate this?' He kissed her tenderly again.

'Yes I do. You're a lousy kisser as well.'

He rolled off and lay beside her, supporting himself on his elbow. Now he stroked her belly then ran his fingers down her waist and over her pubis. As he caressed the golden pelt and slipped his hand between her legs, energy pulsed to her nub.

'Arsehole,' she sighed, but worked her hips.

As he started to stroke the inner surface of her thigh, it quivered. And when his finger slipped through the furrow of her pussy, a shudder of delight ran through her body.

'Pig,' she whispered, and raised her pelvis.

He pressed his lips to hers and his finger began to stroke her slowly, tickling her clitoris underneath so that it stood out from its hood. The finger slipped so easily, and her hips kept up their rhythm.

Now she turned to touch him too, bending her leg to give him open access to herself. Her hand slid to his crotch as she kissed him.

He took a sharp breath and drove his middle finger deep into her vulva, the others digging into the membranes of her loins.

A charge of energy was building in her lower body now. She could feel its heat, spreading up to her breasts and down to her secret lips. She had fantasised about this man for so long and now he was touching her there.

It had been an illogical attraction. His way of life and the ethics of his company, Bentonne Universal, were diametrically opposed to hers. But now she was undoing his belt and slipping his zip, and smiling as she found that he wore no pants. As her fingers felt the heat of his shaft, they curled and began to work it gently, trembling at the touch. It had been so long since she'd felt a man's cock stiffen in her fingers.

She closed her eyes as his mouth came down to hers once more and his long finger began to penetrate her so strongly that she writhed. Urgently now she worked his foreskin, delighting at its silkiness gliding on the helmet of his glans. Her fingers slipped downward, feeling the veins of his stiff shaft as they throbbed to his rapid pulse.

The whole of his hand worked the lips of her vulva now, the middle finger still doing the job her body wanted his shaft to do. But her mind said no – not yet.

As he thrust his tongue into her mouth, imitating the action of his finger, Jodi felt her climax almost come. Quickly, her fingers pushed his shorts right down. As he kicked them and his trainers off she swallowed hard. He had such powerful legs, and such a brute of a cock, its velvety tip turning purple as she drove the foreskin down. She fondled his testes, heavy but mobile in her palm.

'My god, Jodi,' he moaned. 'That's wonderful. You're a witch.'

She raised herself on one elbow and pushed him on to his back, reluctantly losing contact with his finger. Another few seconds of that fingering would have brought her climax on and she did not want that yet.

Her mouth came down to his for a couple of seconds. Then as her hand worked gently at his balls, juggling with her fingers she whispered to his lips, 'And you're sad prick, Bentonne.'

He stroked her hair. 'You're not still angry with me, are you, sweetheart?'

She grimaced. 'Angry? No – I'm bloody furious. And I'll teach you to fool around with me.' Her fingers ringed his testes and as she squeezed, his face went pale.

'Move a muscle, "sweetheart",' she hissed through her teeth as she twisted her grip, 'and you'll be singing like a choirboy.'

He lay still, looking angrily up into her eyes but saying nothing.

Jodi's heart was racing. The feel of his testes in her hand and the stiff shaft springing against her arm was sending her senses wild. It gave her a sense of power she had never had before. Her animal instinct was to take his cock in her mouth. Her vulval lips were throbbing, and she was so hot and moist and ready that she didn't know how long she could hold out before she let him take her. But for now, she had him where she wanted him, and it was marvellous.

'Now, Mr Bentonne,' she whispered. 'It's your turn to answer some questions.'

'Go to hell, Barens.'

She smiled at the way the tables had turned. 'I probably shall go to hell. How I allowed myself to get into this mess I shall never know. But I do know that I'm not going to stay here for your pleasure then be made to disappear mysteriously. Now – where did you put my clothes?'

He nodded behind her.

Jodi turned her head to see her things on a clothes horse by the fire. She also noticed a folding ladder coming from a loft door in the ceiling. So there was a secret attic. Perhaps he had his girlfriend hidden there. She stopped herself. That was wild and illogical. Her mind was creating fantasies again.

'How do you think you're going to get away?' he croaked.

His question brought her attention back to her hand.

She only had to apply the slightest pressure to make him flinch.

He scowled. 'You'll have to let go of me while you dress. And even if you manage to escape, don't think I won't come after you.'

She almost climaxed as she twisted his sac. She was becoming an animal and wanted desperately to mate. Was this what sadism did to people? That's what had happened with that fool who'd written the letter. He'd taken to spanking her while he'd had her from behind. The problem was, she'd liked it. It had given her such a charge she'd tingled all over for hours. But now she was getting an even bigger thrill from holding Bentonne by the balls.

He shifted his position, his shaft stiffening as he raised his hips.

'I told you not to move.' She gave him a cautionary squeeze. He lay quietly, but she could see that he was seething. Once she let him go, he would turn on her. Was that what she wanted? Was there something perverse in her that needed anger from a man? He had been so raunchy in the forest – and she had been disappointed that he had not thrown her in the grass and had her.

'You'll have to let me go soon, Jodi.'

'Shut up. I'm thinking.' She gave his scrotum a tug to reinforce her words while she racked her brains to form a plan of escape. But first she needed information; otherwise the whole mission would have been a waste of time and she wouldn't get paid. She wasn't quite sure which would be worse, Bentonne's anger or the client's.

Bentonne winced as she inadvertently squeezed him.

'Jodi, you're hurting me.'

She grinned. 'Good. You deserve it. Now tell me just what the hell is going on. A busy man like you doesn't swan around naked in the forest unless there's some strong attraction.'

He shifted again. 'Look – if I tell you why I'm here, will you let go of my balls?'

She looked at him askance. 'Let them go so that you can pounce on me? Get real.'

He shook his head. 'It seems that we've both got questions to be answered. Why don't we pool our information and work together?' His eyes began to gleam and a smile came to his lips. 'I'll tell you my problems, and you tell me who sent you here to spy. I don't believe you're here just to catch me misbehaving.'

'So you have been fooling around.'

'I didn't say that. My god, you read so much into things.'

Jodi's hand was getting cramp. She relaxed her grip slightly. 'Are you suggesting a truce?'

He nodded. 'I think that would be wise. I hope you realise now that I really wouldn't hurt you.'

'And you'll tell me why you're playing Pan in the woods when you should damned well be working to create better conditions for your Third World workers.'

'I'm not a playboy, Jodi. I work extremely hard. And even though you might not think so, I do care about our workers.'

As Jodi relaxed her grip, her fingers began to fondle him, lifting his testes and letting them drop.

He let out a sigh of relief, or was it pleasure? She didn't care. All she knew was that she was fed up of the cat-and-mouse game they'd been playing.

His penis stiffened as she stroked it, rolling down the foreskin to make the helmet swell. The charge in her abdomen was creating a pressure now, opening out her secret lips.

Suddenly he rolled.

She yelped and tried to push him off but he caught her arms and pinned them to her sides. Then she felt his shaft as he thrust it deep inside her, filling her in a trice.

Chapter Four

BENTONNE'S THRUST WAS so unexpected it made Jodi cry out. She tried to close her legs, but he was far too strong for her and she was so slippery that he filled her her in a fraction of a second.

'Fucking monster!' She spat in his face. 'You lousy bastard. I thought I could trust you.'

He grinned with triumph. 'Never trust a man when you're playing with his cock, Miss Barens. Now – let's continue our discussion more sensibly, shall we?

'Go to hell.'

He grinned. 'Not until I've got the information I want from you.'

'I don't know any more than I've told you.' A wave of pleasure ran through her as he worked himself deeply in her a few times, closing his eyes in ecstasy as he thrust. Then he looked down earnestly.

'Look, Jodi, I know that you were sent here by my cousin Maximillian. So you might as well admit to it and save yourself a lot of trouble.'

She shook her head. 'Your cousin who?'

'Come now, don't play the dumb blonde with me. It was he who commissioned you to come here spying, wasn't it?'

'You're barking up the wrong tree, Bentonne. I—'

He drove into her hard several times, grinding his pubis against hers, crushing her clitoris to send darts of pleasure/pain shooting through her body.

She gasped as he bit her neck, then forced her legs wide by bringing up his knees, stretching her membranes taut and opening up the mouth of her sex.

'My god, you're a brute,' she whispered. 'But don't think you'll get any more from me than I've already told you. I don't give in that easily.'

Jodi trembled all over. Having him in the centre of her need felt so good. She knew that nothing else would release the tension that had been building over the past two hours. When she wriggled as if to get away, it only made her want it more.

He kissed her nose. 'Spirited little thing, aren't you? And so wonderfully tight.'

'Don't be crude.'

He worked himself slowly in her, almost drawing out before filling her again.

Jodi curled her legs around his hips. This way she presented herself widely to him. All he would have to do to bring her to completion was to drive down several times, pressing the root of his penis hard against her nub.

As he stopped his movement and studied her face, she could feel the weight of his testes tickling at her secret lips, and wriggled to feel them better.

'Don't stop now,' she whispered as much to herself as to him. 'I can't stand your teasing any longer.'

He bit her neck. 'Tell me who your client is, and I'll fuck you any way you like.' He gave her a few hard thrusts as if to emphasise his condition.

Jodi sighed. This was getting wearing. 'Look – I got the job through my usual agency. They don't always tell me who the client is, or why he wants a surveillance done. And I've never heard of anybody called Maximillian. Now – are you satisfied?'

'Not fully satisfied,' he whispered as he took her mouth and kissed her gently. 'If you're not working for Maximillian, I don't understand why you were told to follow me. There's no scandal for you. All I'm doing is relaxing alone while I work out some business stratetgies.'

He looked as if he was telling the truth, but already he had tricked her more than once. So she decided not to trust him. She would have to string him along and find out what was really going on.

Without warning, he drew out of her and stood up, his penis slick with her moisture, glowing in the firelight. She looked up at him, his legs set apart, the weight of his testes dragging at his sac. She wanted to kiss it; to feel its softness against her lips. Instead she sat up and glowered.

'What the hell are you doing now?'

'I'm going to get some stew. I'm famished.'

'But what about me?' She stood up and faced him.

'Don't worry – you can have some stew as well.'

She slapped his hand away as he toyed with her nipple. 'I didn't mean that. I meant . . .'

'I know what you meant. But you'll have to wait. I'm trying to decide which of your offers to accept.'

'What "offers"?'

'You said I might tie you while I whip you. Or have you over the kitchen table while I spank you like your boyfriend did.' He grinned widely and went into the kitchen, and soon returned with two bowls of stew.

They ate in silence, mopping up the gravy with chunks of bread. Bentonne stood before her, still naked and quite unashamed. He was magnificent, and despite his sarcasm and his treachery, she still wanted him. She wanted him to throw her on the bed and take her like an animal.

'Jodi?'

Dragged away from the sensation of energy coursing though her, Jodi's attention snapped to his face.

'What now?'

'Jodi, what ambitions do you have?'

She shrugged noncommittally. 'Why?'

'I wondered why you do the job you do.'

'And wouldn't I be better doing something more constructive?' she finished for him, with a sneer.

He ignored it. 'Most people have ambitions to do something worthwhile with their lives.'

'Most people are handicapped by lack of money or time. But that doesn't apply to you, does it?'

As Bentonne studied her, Jodi could sense that he was fishing for something. She was on her guard.

He finished up his stew. 'I suppose I am more fortunate than most people.'

'You're damned right you are. Have you ever wondered why?'

'Tell me.' He looked at her with surprise.

'All right. I will. How do people like you get so much money?'

'We work hard for it.'

'Huh!' She threw her head back, her hair flouncing over her shoulder, shining gold now in the bright light from the fire. 'You don't have to work as hard as the poor devils who graft in your diamond mines, the gold mines, the tea and rubber plantations, the mills and god knows what other enterprises of Bentonne Universal. I've seen the squalor where such workers live, the poverty that people like you create while you live like kings.'

'Like this, do you mean?' He gestured towards the sparse little room.

That nearly floored her. These surroundings were in a time warp. But she was in full spate now, so she ignored the remark.

'Don't evade the issue. Do you deny that your family's money has been made by breaking the backs of countless thousands of serfs for a century or more? Do you deny that your companies thrive in Third World countries because labour is so cheap and laws on environmental pollution are so lax?'

His face was expressionless, but she could see an intensity of interest in his eyes which she found curious. She had expected anger.

'Well? Do you?'

'Why should I deny it? It's true. But I am trying to change it.'

'I'll believe that when I see it.'

He shrugged. 'Believe what you like.'

She pulled herself up sharply, glaring at him. It allowed her anger to boil over, and she gave no thought to how violently he might react.

'You asked me if I had an ambition. Well, I do have. It's to see people like you made to pay proper wages, and to provide decent living conditions for their workers. I want to see you put your money into healing the planet, not destroying it for greed. Anything I can do to make that happen, I will.'

Bentonne continued to watch her intensely but said nothing. That made her more annoyed.

She put her fists on her hips, caring little that her breasts were thrusting, or that she was hot with the need he'd generated in her and denied again. He'd probably done it to pay her back for what she'd done to him.

He had not defended himself against her tirade. All he had done was stand there looking cool, raunchy and pulsing with virility. She wanted to slap his face, but wanted to have him too. Damn! He had her in such a whirl, and all he did was look at her.

A rumble of thunder cut into Jodi's thoughts. Her heart sank. 'I need to get my camera in. I don't want it wrecked in another storm.'

Dean paused for a moment, then picked up her clothes and went to the door. She rose to go with him but he put up his hand.

'Don't move a muscle. I'll be back in two minutes. But I'll take these for security, so don't think of running off.' The lock ground from the outside.

Jodi fumed, her arms clamped hard across her breasts. The man was impossible. He was a pig. She could not stand such treatment for much longer.

The wood fire crackled, sending sparklets soaring up the flue. The oil lamp at the ceiling lit the room dimly with its flicker. Jodi looked at the folding ladder going into the darkness of the loft. Did he intend to imprison her up there?

Quickly, she crept up the ladder, her ankle stronger since the swelling had gone down. She penetrated the blackness through the trap-door, but she could see nothing. Then something brushed her cheek. Putting out her hand to push it away, she found that it was the cord of a pull switch. Her heart pounded, and her hand trembled as she pulled. Her eyes were ready to see old furniture, cobwebs, and the grime of a couple of hundred years.

As the switch clicked, the attic space was flooded with a brilliant glare. It took a few seconds for Jodi's eyes to become accustomed to the brightness. When a picture did develop, she gasped.

The space was high enough to stand in at the centre. The walls were panelled in white, the floor covered in a thick green carpet. Unexpectedly cool, it seemed to be air-conditioned. Around the edges were stainless steel desks, each supporting high-technology equipment. Video screens glowed green beside keyboards and printers. A fax machine blinked.

While Jodi's feet stood in a Victorian world, her head was in the space age.

The lights of a printer flickered as it silently spewed out a stream of closely printed paper. On one screen, a bar of light swept round, picking up bright dots on its journey.

The biggest surprise was delivered by a black-and-white monitor close to Jodi's head. It displayed a view around the outside of the house as if the camera was taking the shot from the chimney stack. The image must have been electronically enhanced since it showed the area clearly in the dim light. When she saw Bentonne picking up her tripod she groaned. If he'd been watching that screen when she'd set up her gear, he would easily have seen her. So – had he known that she was snapping him as he'd run from the cottage to swim? Had he put on his display with the idea of luring her and finding her with incriminating evidence? Damn! The man was more cunning than she'd given him credit for.

As Bentonne started towards the cottage with Jodi's camera, she dived down into the old world below. Taking her seat in the rocking chair, she sat supping stew when he entered with her camera and equipment bag. She looked up with a weak smile. Expertly, he removed the film cassette from the camera and threw it in the fire. Jodi frowned as it flared but made a performance of eating stew, trying to give the impression that she had been fully occupied with that while he'd been away, though her pulse raced madly.

He looked at her, then at the ladder. She tried to ignore his visual enquiry as if she was totally innocent of any misdemeanour. But when he climbed the ladder and switched off the light she felt the heat of a blush creep slowly up her neck. He pushed the ladder upward, folding it into the ceiling. A textured board attached to it fitted exactly into the hole between two beams. Now there was no sign that there was any ladder, any hole, or any high-tech control room.

Jodi lowered her eyes as he stood before her, his penis flaccid again, the foreskin rolled right back to expose the glans. His belly heaved with exertion, making the organ swing. His expression was hard.

'So you did come to spy. I knew you were lying. I suppose they thought if they sent an attractive woman, I wouldn't suspect anything.'

She stood to face him. 'That's not true. I was only told to tail you, not to check your toys up there.' She nodded to the loft. 'I know I shouldn't have been nosy, but . . .'

He pinched her face, his eyes angry. 'And now that you know my secret, I suppose you think you'll go running home to blab it to my cousin, Maximillian?'

She pulled away, frightened. 'I told you before, I don't know anything about your cousin.' Then a spark of self-righteousness lit the fire of independence in her. 'Anyway – if you didn't want me to see that room, you shouldn't have left the ladder down.'

'That was a test, you little fool. And you failed it.'

She'd have to brave it out. 'Too bad. But why the secrecy? If you're not doing something illegal, why hide it in a place like this?'

Dean reflected for a moment. 'All right – I'll tell you, but it won't do you any good. That facility is my way of

49

keeping tabs on Bentonne Universal without anybody realising they're being monitored. The equipment is connected by satellite to the offices of every subsidiary company. I get data direct from their computers and from trusted employees.'

Jodi threw her head back righteously. 'And you accused *me* of spying!'

His face was grim as he contemplated her. 'But I have the right to find out who's robbing the company blind.'

She shrugged. 'If you weren't starving the employees, maybe they wouldn't steal the paper clips.'

'Don't be sarcastic, Barens. It doesn't suit you.'

The remark made her feel small and she glowered.

He seemed not to notice. 'And, for your information, it's more than paper clips being stolen. The deficit runs to millions. If it continues, the company might fold. Then where will your poor workers be?'

'OK – I'm sorry. I didn't mean to be flippant. Who's the embezzler?'

'If I could prove that, I wouldn't be trying to squeeze the information out of you, would I? I'm sure your appearance here is connected in some way.' There was a note of sarcasm in his voice and it made her go cold. For a moment she had thought that he liked her; now she wasn't sure. And for some crazy reason it mattered. She realised that she'd been a fool to fall into his trap. Now, with so much money involved, only god knew what Dean might do to shut her up.

The fire flickered in unison with the oil lamp. In that Victorian world, the room above might have been a figment of Jodi's imagination. The whole situation was a conundrum.

She moved in close, running a forefinger down Dean's chest. 'Look, Dean. I said I'm sorry about peeking in your attic. I won't tell a soul, honestly.' He tried to push her away, but she held his arms. 'Please don't be angry with me.' She looked into his eyes then reached up to kiss his lips.

He did not respond.

She slipped her arms around his waist and pushed her breasts against his chest, her cheek against his neck. She could feel his heat through her nipples. His buttocks were rigid under her palms as she stroked them, trying to coax some life into him. He'd been so playful earlier.

Still he didn't move. 'You won't get round me like this, Miss Barens.'

'Why would I want to get round you? You haven't got anything I particularly want.' She smiled to herself and sank to her knees, her lips kissing at his chest, his abdomen and pubis.

His rising penis came up against her chin. She licked his testes, just as she had wanted to do when the rain drops were running off them. Then she ran her tongue up the centre of his cock, savouring its aroma. She took it in one hand and fed it into her mouth, closing her eyes as she closed her lips upon it.

His cock went hard in the heat of her mouth, and he gave a murmur of appreciation as he thrust his pelvis forward.

She began to plunge down on it, and he quivered to her touch. In any second she was sure that he would spurt.

He ran his fingers through her hair and pulled her to himself. 'My god, Jodi Barens, you're a witch. Do that any more and I'll have to fuck you,' he sighed.

'Threats like that will get you where I want you to be,' she whispered, and plunged her mouth down on him again. Pulling away, she bared the helmet of his cock, which glistened with her saliva, and licked it

51

slowly around the rim, making it pulse to every lap.

He thrust into her mouth, whispering, 'Does this mean that we're friends again?'

She looked up across his belly. 'If that's what you want.'

'Then shall we join forces and find out who sent you to spy on me?'

She stroked the inside of his thigh, then cupped his balls. 'OK. But if I cooperate with you, you must promise to reform.'

'In what way?'

'Change the way you run your companies so the workers get a fairer deal.'

He smiled. 'Agreed. But I have to get control first.'

She rubbed her finger up and down his shaft. 'But aren't you Chief Executive?'

He pushed his shaft into her mouth, closing his eyes as she sucked it. 'I was only acting Chief Exec while my father was ill. He's decided to step down, and the job's up for grabs.'

Jodi pulled away reluctantly. 'But aren't you the heir to the family business?'

He shook his head and tried to push into her mouth again. She resisted, determined to get an answer to her question.

He stroked her cheeks as he pushed his cock against her lips. 'I'm not the only one who wants the job, Jodi. My cousin Maximillian, on my mother's side of the family, is very ambitious.'

To reward him for giving her the data, Jodi opened her mouth and let him push his penis in. He closed his eyes, relishing the sensation of her tongue against his glans while he spoke. 'Max and I have always been deadly rivals. Now that my father is standing down, Max is vying with me for control.'

She nodded, sucking on him slowly, trying not to let her attention wander too much from the subject. The way he was pushing was making her more aroused.

She pulled away reluctantly. 'So who decides which of you should be the boss?'

'The Board.' He ran a finger down her neck.

She widened her knees so that she could rub her clitoris to heighten her arousal. Heck, she wanted him so badly . . . But she needed the information more. Clearly there was more to this matter than checking on Bentonne's alleged infidelity.

'What exactly is this Board?'

'They're the Directors of the Company, mostly old men with very puritanical ideas.'

'What do you mean,"puritanical"?' She pressed down with her tongue on the web of his glans, stretching his foreskin and making his phallus rear up before her.

'They're very old-fashioned.'

'In what way?'

'They expect directors to be whiter than white. At the slightest hint of scandal, they're out.'

'And is your cousin whiter than white?'

Bentonne threw his head back and laughed, jogging his cock against her cheek, painting it with her own saliva. 'No, he's not. Maximillian is a womaniser.'

'And you aren't, I suppose?'

'You're the first woman I've touched for well over a year. I've been very careful not to be seen on my own with any woman, or in any compromising situation.'

'So that's why you're so horny.'

He didn't answer that.

She took his testes one by one and sucked them, then looked up across his belly. His eyes were closed and he was breathing hard.

'So, if this cousin of yours is a lecher, why are they considering him for Chief Executive?'

'Because he lies his way out of any awkward situation, and the Board think the sun shines out of his backside.'

'So are you afraid they'll appoint him instead of you?'

'They won't if I can prove he's been stealing from the firm.'

'And what if you can't prove that?'

He smiled grimly. 'I have to. I know he's been smuggling gold from our South African mines, but I still haven't found out how it's done. I'm monitoring every move he makes. He only needs to make one mistake and I've got him.'

Bentonne pushed his penis out for her to suck. 'But if Maximillian suspects I'm gathering information on his crooked dealings, he'll be frantic to find out what I know. He might go to any lengths to stop me being appointed instead of him. And that, my dear Miss Barens, is why you have to stay here until after the board meeting in three days' time.'

Jodi squatted, looking at the cock rearing in front of her. The whole of her body was shaking with the tension the sight was creating, and she couldn't wait much longer to satisfy her desire.

'But if it was your cousin who hired me through my agent, I wasn't briefed to look for any fancy apparatus in your attic. I don't know anything about computers or . . .'

He pushed his penis down and slipped it into her mouth, making her swallow hard. As she squatted before him, the tightly stretched membranes inside her thighs began to tremble uncontrollably. Who the hell cared who ran Bentonne Universal? Right now, all she wanted was her climax.

As he eased her to the mat, her body went quite limp. The heat of the fire upon her breasts and belly added even more to her internal heat.

She pulled back her legs and spread herself as he knelt and looked between them. She always got a surge when a man looked at her down there.

The thunder growled and rain began to patter on the window. The light of the smoky oil lamp danced upon her skin.

'Thanks for telling me,' she said softly as he ran a finger up the inside of her leg, over one lip of her pussy and down the other side. 'I swear I didn't know anything about your problems with your cousin. I promise I won't tell anyone.'

He smiled as he circled her nubbin with one finger. 'I know you won't. I'm going to keep you fully occupied here until I've sorted cousin Maxi out, and been elected Chief Exec. I'm not risking you throwing a spanner in the works.' He pushed her knees back firmly and lay between her legs.

'And if I don't agree?'

When his mouth reached her pussy, she felt his tongue parting her. Then he licked her very slowly from her nubbin to her navel, right up to her chin.

He buttressed his arms beside her breasts and grinned down at her. 'You have no choice, Miss Barens. You're my prisoner. And if you're a naughty girl and try to get away again, I'll have to tie you up and spank your lovely bottom while I fuck you from behind like your boyfriend did.' He grinned that boyish grin, which turned her to jelly without fail.

Jodi felt heat flush to her cheeks. 'Then I'll have to try to escape.' She smiled coyly and pulled back her legs.

The thunder rolled again.

Jodi's lubrication welled as Dean bowed his back and thrust inside her deeply.

The searing flash that lit the room made her blink.

Bentonne penetrated her fully as he glanced towards the window. Jodi expected to hear thunder follow the flash, but it did not come.

Bentonne looked down at his shaft as he drew it out and let it nose about her labia, teasing her by rubbing it against her clitoris. Then he watched it disappear as he slid it into her again, very, very slowly.

'Stop it,' she hissed. 'If you're going to fuck me at all, then fuck me properly.' She pushed her knees apart to stretch herself. He took her strongly and soon began to pant. But when he tensed, she cried out, 'No!' It was too soon for him to come.

There was another flash and, this time, the unmistakable click and whirr of the film-winding mechanism of a camera.

As Bentonne ripped himself from her she felt the warmth of semen on her belly. When he sprang to his feet, a spurt shot in the air and fell between her legs, trickling through her furrow.

The third flash blinded Jodi. Black dots swam in her vision for several seconds before she recovered her senses and sat. Petrified, she stared up at Bentonne.

Incredulity, then anger, and then rage rushed though his eyes. Towering over her, he snarled. 'You bloody, scheming bitch!' The flat of his hand cracked across her face, jolting it sideways with the force. 'You planned this from the start, didn't you! And just as I was beginning to trust you . . .'

Chapter Five

WITH ONE BLOW, Dean Bentonne destroyed every-thing that had been building between Jodi and himself.

Jodi sank to the floor, absolutely stunned. Her face stung from his slap. She looked up with disbelief, croak-ing, 'Dean, you've got to believe me! I didn't have anything to do with this.' What she saw shocked her more than the blow had done: there was hatred in his eyes.

'You slut. I wondered how low you might stoop to get what you wanted, but I was fool enough to let you lower my defences.'

'No, that's not true. I—' She put out a defending hand as he tugged her to her feet, cutting her sentence in mid air. Then he pulled her towards the doorway and thrust her out. But as she was dragged into the balmy night, she began to recover from the total shock and her anger rose. She pulled her hand from Bentonne's grasp and snapped, 'I'm not going without my camera gear or my clothes.'

'You're coming with me.'

She felt the fire of anger rush up to her cheeks as she made a motion to go back into the cottage. But Bentonne shot out an arm and roughly snatched her back.

'We're going to catch your accomplice before he reaches the main road.'

'Look, Bentonne,' Jodi began, but he would not listen as he dragged her to the jeep she had seen earlier in the lean-to. It had two flat rear tyres.

Bentonne turned on her, snarling. 'Your accomplice has done a thorough job, hasn't he? He didn't take the risk of getting caught when he left you behind. I suppose he thought I wouldn't hurt you if he deserted you. Well, I'll hurt him when I catch up with him.'

Bentonne thrust Jodi into the jeep. She tried to resist but knew that she would be no match for him in a fight, especially as her ankle was still sore and she could not run.

He started the engine, turning to her with a wry smile. 'Two flat tyres won't stop me, Barens.'

They roared off across the clearing, the jeep slewing in the ruts of the forest track. Jodi hung on to the driver's seat with one hand and to the windscreen with the other. As she gripped both with all the strength that she could summon, her breasts bounced freely. The vehicle ploughed among the trees, missing one by the thickness of a coat of paint.

As Jodi shot a glance at Bentonne she saw a frightening image. He was a totally different man from the one she had made love to by the fire. He was steel-hard, his face set rigid. The determination she read there meant that he was certainly not a man to be toyed with, and she concluded that she was now seeing the true side of the Bentonne nature. Part of her thrilled; part of her was scared.

'Dean . . .'

'Shut up and hang on.'

But Jodi would not be shut up. She shouted against the screaming engine as she pounded his naked shoulder with her fist, 'Listen to me, you fool!' She would not be put down by the man. 'This has nothing to do with me. I didn't know anything about it.'

Bentonne drove as if a herd of charging wildebeest was inches from his rear. 'If your friend's still inside the forest, I've got him,' he shouted, not taking his attention from his driving for a second.

The track was only dimly lit by the headlamps of the jeep. It was a marvel to Jodi that they did not crash. Then, up ahead she saw the rear lights of another vehicle on the track.

Bentonne swerved to one side and took another, even rougher track. Now they were keeping pace with the other lights. Flashing between the trees, they seemed to be converging.

As they shot from the forest on to a gravel roadway, the jeep squirmed on the loose surface, the rear tyres flapping at the rims. Then, as both vehicles reached a fork, Bentonne threw the jeep across the path of a large, black van. Jodi shielded her eyes from the headlamp's glare as Bentonne sprang out and grabbed a double-barrelled gun from the jeep. Then he dragged the driver from the van, flinging him roughly against a tree and raising the gun to his chest.

Jodi was surprised to see that the driver was a fair-haired youth. Handsome and tall, he was nineteen at the most. In the brightness of the headlights, Jodi recognised him immediately as he scanned her nakedness with a mischievous look in his clear, blue eyes. She had bumped into him in her agent's office a couple of weeks before. Now she knew she'd been set up. When she saw a camera slung over his shoulder, it was enough to make her really angry.

Jumping from the jeep, she completely forgot her nudity, interested only in hearing what the fellow had to say. Bentonne faced him with the shotgun, his legs apart, his testes swinging loosely as his belly pumped for breath.

'You scum,' he barked. 'I don't know what you think you'll gain by snapping me with her. The press won't touch material like that.'

The youth didn't respond, except to push a shock of thick, fair hair back from his forehead.

Bentonne glowered as he snatched the camera. Then turning to Jodi, he grabbed her arm and pushed her at the youth.

She shrank away in horror as she was caught by strong arms and held. She stared back at Bentonne with disbelief as he raised the gun to cover them and snatched up a mobile phone from the jeep. Pressing the nine three times with his thumb, he barked what sounded like a coded message, then threw the phone back into the jeep. He took a menacing pace towards them.

'Now – while we wait for the police, you two might as well tell me who you're working for.'

The young man seemed to gain in confidence now that he had Jodi as a shield. 'Ask Jodi,' he whispered as he kissed her neck. 'Are you all right, lover? I hope the brute didn't hurt you.'

Jodi looked over her shoulder with horror. She struggled but could not get away.

Bentonne glowered at Jodi. 'So you were lying all along, you slut. Now I don't think there's any doubt that you're both working for my cousin.'

'I told you I had nothing to do with this, Bentonne. I—'

Her captor broke her sentence as he said loudly enough for Bentonne to hear, 'Don't worry, sweetheart, I won't let him have you again.' He kissed her neck and fanned his hands across her belly.

She shook her head wildly. 'Don't listen to him, Dean! I don't know him.' She tried to get away again but the youth held her tightly, her breasts pushed out by his arms, the heat of his chest against her bare back. And she thought that she could feel his erection against the crevice of her bottom.

'Save your lies,' Bentonne snarled. 'And I'll make damned sure the police throw the book at you.'

Jodi felt sick as she glared at Bentonne. She was not going to be associated with the youth or his smutty game, whatever that might be. But how would she prove her innocence?

She kicked her captor on the shin and made him yelp. Then she broke from his grip and started to walk away, her head held high.

'Where the hell do you think you're going?' Bentonne growled, and grabbed her arm.

She shook him off and spat, 'I'm leaving. I'm not one of your minions to order around.' With Bentonne standing naked in the headlights, and the young man's blue eyes on her breasts, adrenaline was running through her body like a fire rushing through dry tinder.

As Bentonne held the gun on her, she passed him with her head held up.

'Jodi. Jodi!' he barked. Come back here or I swear I'll . . .'

She didn't stop, even though she was not totally certain if she would hear the sound of a gun and feel the searing heat of pellets in her back. Just to show defiance, she turned and shouted over her shoulder, 'You can both go to hell.' But as she turned back, she stopped dead in her tracks. A huge man blocked her way, his square face mangled like a veteran boxer's, his small deep-set black eyes scanning her lasciviously. He wore a black boiler suit with sleeves four inches too short; one hand hung ape-like at his side, the other held a pistol.

Jodi pulled herself together. 'Who the hell are you?'

The man's eyes narrowed. 'Dat none of your business.' He gestured to her to turn and pushed her roughly back towards Bentonne. Pointing to the jeep, he barked, 'Get dat out of way!'

Jodi looked from one man to the other and thought she saw fear in Bentonne's eyes. She froze when the big man took her neck in an iron-hard grip and growled at Bentonne, 'You move dat or I hurt der woman.'

The words struck cold into Jodi's heart but then her anger came to life. She elbowed him hard in the belly, but he only gripped her harder, whispering in her ear, 'I like woman with spirit. I think I take you home with me.' And then he laughed a laugh that welled up from his belly.

As a police siren sounded in the distance, Bentonne sprang forward in Jodi's defence. But he stopped in his tracks as she felt the coldness of the pistol at her temple. Her attention was now split between Bentonne and the gun; the painful grip on her neck made her wriggle, but she could not shake it off. The image of Dean Bentonne blurred.

The siren of the police car sounded again. Would they arrive to find her lying dead among the bushes? Who would miss her? The landlord? She hadn't paid her rent. And she owed the man at the corner shop for a month's supplies. And – hell, this was crazy. She was about to be murdered and all she could think about was her grocery bill.

She kicked out hard at her captor's shins as he tightened his grip around her neck. With no shoes on her feet, it did no good at all. As he shoved her forward, she saw Dean Bentonne in a haze, moving as if in slow motion. He was getting into the jeep. Her knees began to give way.

The next few seconds were a blur. She was thrown into the van to land on a pile of sacks. Bentonne crashed down beside her, his elbow jabbing into her side, taking away her breath. The clang of metal doors, the roar of the engine and the squeal of tyres followed in fast succession. Then Jodi's world went black. She was no longer interested in anything, least of all Bentonne's vendetta with his cousin.

Jodi became aware that she was being carried over someone's shoulder. Her heart sank. Her mind raced in an effort to recall what had happened last. Her memories seemed hazy, as if events had taken place in a dream. But the bump, bump of her stomach on the shoulder was no dream. Neither was the ground slipping dizzily past her eyes. Her wrists were tied in front of her, her arms hanging down the man's back, her nipples chafing at his boiler suit. Still completely naked, she was very aware of a warm breeze between her legs as her captor marched.

She strained in the darkness to see her surroundings. The ground looked black like the bitumen surface of a car park. Not daring to look up, she moved her head to one side and caught a glimpse of Bentonne walking beside her bearer. The gun was pressed between his shoulders, held by the young, blond man. To her dismay Bentonne's hands were tied behind his back.

Jodi's sensitive nose picked up a scent, and her experience of light aircraft told her it was aviation fuel. An engine ground on its starter. She felt a warm breeze from a propeller as blades blurred into a ring. A wave of despondency washed through her mind: there was little chance of escape from a plane.

The legs of her captor stopped at metal steps. Off to one side, Jodi spotted a torpedo-shaped object hanging from a wing. Whipping her head round to the other side, she caught a quick glimpse of the aircraft's registration letters: G W F. 'Golly What Fun,' she whispered to herself as she automatically recorded the letters. But she couldn't read the letter that came before the G as she was dumped on the floor of the plane. She fell on something soft; Bentonne gasped out 'Careful!'

'Sorry.' Jodi's apology was automatic. But she bit her lip. She wasn't really sorry and would not apologise to him after what he'd done to her. She still seethed at his disbelief of her story. And she smarted inwardly at the way he'd struck her. Her cheek was bruised as well as her pride. A sharp voice took her attention. 'She wake up.' The big man's accent caught Jodi's attention. She could not quite place it until he said in Dutch with a thick Amsterdam accent, 'Check her bonds – I don't want her to try anything heroic.'

Jodi smiled thinly. That was the first bit of luck she'd had since she had been caught by Bentonne in the woods. She grimaced at the big man who stood framed in a small door opening, looking at her breasts.

Spontaneously, she spat, making him stand back quickly.

'I would not be rude to Mr Polders, Miss Barens,' the young man said softly in almost perfect English. 'He is not very nice to people he does not like. At present, he likes you very much, don't you, Mr Polders?'

The big man's eyes glinted as he smiled and eyed her mons. The idea of Mr Polders liking her in any way at all, was quite repulsive, although perversely she found the blond man attractive in a boyish way. He spread thick blankets over them, shrugged remorsefully, then whispered, 'I'm sorry to do this to you Jodi, but now

64

you can identify us, we cannot take the risk of letting you go.'

The door was shut and the engines revved. The floor bumped them violently as the plane taxied. Eventually it took off after what seemed to be a very long run.

Accustomed to light aircraft for covering large areas of South African veldt, Jodi speculated on what she had seen. It was a twin-engined four-seater. By the narrowness of the tapering space, she knew they were in a small luggage compartment behind the main cabin. From the way the aircraft flew and the straining throb of the engines, she guessed that it was nearing its load limit. Apart from her two captors there was perhaps a small payload too. Carried as baggage, she and Bentonne would be alone and unguarded until they landed – or were ditched into the sea. She shivered at the thought.

Jodi snuggled under the blankets and moved towards Bentonne's warmth, trying to make out which part of him she was touching. Her face came up against his shoulder and her breasts against his chest as he lay on his side. She felt his thigh with her bound hands, then found his testes with her fingers.

'Ouch. Be careful where you put your hands.'

'Shut up,' she hissed and nudged him again, getting curious satisfaction out of his reaction. Then she relented. 'Are you OK?'

'Oh yes, I'm having a wonderful time, no thanks to you.'

'I told you, this has nothing to do with me.'

'Bullshit. The boy knew your name.'

'He was in cahoots with my agent. That bastard must have set me up.'

'You don't expect me to believe that, do you?'

Jodi fumed. Bentonne was such a prig. 'I suppose

you would only have believed me if that man with the pistol had blown my head off.'

'He was only pretending he might shoot you.'

'So – if you thought that, why did you look so worried about me?'

'I was worried about them leaving someone behind to ransack the cottage, not about you, Barens.'

Despite her anger at him, the remark hurt Jodi deeply. At one point in the cottage she had really thought that he had liked her. She had certainly been attracted to him. In future she would not take jobs that had any emotional component. In fact, if she ever got out of this alive, she would go back to tracking big game in the veldt for the tourist companies.

'If you really didn't care anything for me, why did you move the jeep and let them abduct us?' She had to shout in Bentonne's ear, in order to be heard over the drone of the engines.

She heard him let out a breath of exasperation. 'I would have done that for any woman who was being threatened.'

Again she felt let down. In indignation she pushed him in the genitals, surprised to feel that his penis was half hard. Was he stimulated by the situation, or was it simply the vibration of the plane?

'Will you stop it, Jodi? That hurt.'

'Good,' she countered and pushed at him again, partly to annoy him and partly to feel him more. Any man lying beside her with a hard-on seemed to excite her. And he'd called her Jodi. Was he softening towards her? 'I won't stop it until you admit that you did care something for me when you made love to me in the cottage.'

'I found you sexually provocative, if that's what you mean.'

66

'No, it isn't. You said I'm beautiful.'

'That was before you proved you're a double-crossing little bitch.'

'When are you going to get it through your thick skull that I didn't plan any of this!'

He said nothing, and that made her even more mad. So she masturbated him slowly just to spite him. With his hands behind his back he could not stop her.

'Jodi – please don't do that,' he whispered.

'Why not? Have you become celibate all of a sudden?'

He didn't respond but his penis grew erect.

'All right don't answer; but I'll tell you one thing, Bentonne – I'm going to find a way out as soon as this plane lands, and you can play your power games on your own.'

'You surely don't think I like this any more than you do?'

She smirked. 'Like what? Having your cock touched up, or not being able to finish what you started in the cottage?'

'Don't be crass. You know what I mean.'

She sighed, tired of bantering with him. 'OK. So let's call a truce and start being civil to one another.' There was a long silence. 'Are you listening?'

'I heard you.'

'Well then?'

'How do I know you're not still trying to milk me for information?'

She ran his foreskin tightly up and down. 'I think you're paranoid.'

'I am not.'

'Have it your own way. Anyway, what the hell have you done to these characters to make them so hostile?'

There was a long silence before the aircraft suddenly

banked steeply. They slid across the narrow compartment and crashed against the side. Her face ended up against his. The warmth of his belly against her own was making her breathe deeply. Together with the enforced intimacy, the danger was arousing her again. It was crazy, but she could not help how her body reacted to danger.

Bentonne tried to move away but could not.

Jodi was comfortable. He was warm and taut and smelled so stimulating. Images of their intimacy in the cottage flooded through her mind. She smiled wryly to herself as she rubbed his shaft, delighting in the way it stiffened.

'I said stop that, you tart,' he growled.

She did not take her hand from him but lay against him, thinking for a while, her thumb idly fingering the web of his glans. She loved the way this made a man go stiffer, and Bentonne was no exception.

'What happened to the police?' she said after a long silence.

'We passed them just after the van shot off. From the sounds I heard, I think they were forced into a ditch. That henchman of my cousin drove the van with the finesse of a bulldozer.'

'How do you know he's a henchman of your cousin? He could be working for anyone who hates Bentonne Universal.'

'He's Dutch.'

'So?'

'My cousin's Dutch as well.'

'You didn't tell me that before.'

'I assumed that you knew.'

She smarted at the remark and pulled his foreskin sharply.

'Ouch. That hurt, you hellcat!'

'Good. And I'll do it again if you don't stop being such a bloody chauvinist.'

'I was not being—'

She pulled him again. 'Yes you were. You know you were. Now. Tell me what proof you have that cousin Max is swindling your company.'

He laughed, despite the circumstances. 'You're very clever Jodi. I give you full credit for trying.'

'I don't know what you mean.'

He shook his head, his breath fanning on her lips. 'You get yourself shut up with me and play with my cock as brazenly as a whore. Then when you think I'm under your spell again, you ask for proof about my cousin's dirty dealing so you can report to him as soon as we land. And you can tell him from me, he's made the one mistake I was waiting for. When the Board find out about this, they certainly won't elect him.'

'They won't find out about it if your cousin bumps us off before that meeting.'

'My god, you've got a wild imagination, Barens.'

They lapsed into silence for some time before she asked, 'Any ideas about where your cousin might have us taken?'

'You know that already, don't you?'

Jodi ignored his mood and snuggled up to him to get warmer. Even though she was still mad at him, their closeness was a comfort. She ran her fingers down his shaft and pushed her thigh between his legs. His flesh was so firm and warm against her secret lips. She was still tuned up from his toying with her and her failure to climax. Despite her fear during their mad drive through the trees in the jeep, she had thrilled at his physical strength and the determination the man had shown in the face of the enemy. Something in her had succumbed to this power. Perhaps the female in her had submitted to his dominant maleness, her own streak of masculinity taking a rest for once. Despite everything – perhaps *because* of everything – she still wanted him. Apart from anything else, he was a challenge.

Rotating the gold ring on her finger, she struggled with the registration letters she had glimpsed on the fuselage of the plane: G W F. She tried hard to recall any other features she had seen, but her mind would not concentrate. Her body would not let it. The steady beat of Bentonne's pulse in the strong veins of his cock seemed to speed up her own pulse. He wasn't pushing her away now. He was letting her toy with him without protesting.

She smiled to herself as she felt him push his penis through her palm while her mind mulled over all kinds of possibilities for her fate. Perhaps she would be kept as a concubine to Maximillian. Or maybe he would sell her to some white slaver.

Jodi stopped the thoughts. That was ridiculous. Her imagination was running wild again. Hell – this was really serious. Now the devil in her – and her horniness – all conspired to make her slip a finger into the slack skin of his scrotum to pull his foreskin tight.

'What the hell do you think you're doing now, you minx?' Bentonne gasped as she slid her fingers up his shaft and worked the foreskin slowly.

'I'm playing with your prick. And before you protest too loudly, why was it already so stiff when I touched it?'

'I can't help it. It's the vibration.'

'Oh yeah?'

'Yes. Now leave it alone, you slut.'

He was getting angry and it made her thrill. Good. She had him almost where she wanted him. She ran her fingers over his thigh, feeling its tautness, recalling how

70

he had braced his legs as he'd stood before her in the forest. She flexed her fingers gently, making his testes move inside their sac.

He moaned and stretched his legs, making his cock stiffen and curve. She smiled. It was a sign that his body wanted to flex and push that thing inside her. She stroked it gently, letting the vibrations of the plane travel through her fingers to the web of his glans.

'You won't get any more information out of me by doing this, you Jezebel,' he whispered in her ear.

She put her lips to his and whispered through them. 'The only information that I want from you is: are you going to finish what you started at the cottage?'

'You're not serious.'

'I've never been more serious in my life.' She put her lips to his and kissed him slowly. At first he did not respond, but as the vibrations of the aircraft trembled through their lips, he began to move his mouth on hers. Her heart was beating wildly against her breasts, and the gentle undulation of his breathing lulled her into a relaxed state. Her throat was dry again. But the place between her legs where she felt the hardness of his thigh was slippery with her nectar.

'Jodi, we mustn't.'

'Why not? It might be the only chance we get. We might be dead by tomorrow.' She put her mouth to his and kissed him sensuously.

'You're a witch, Barens,' he whispered through the kiss, then took her mouth with passion.

Now she was alight. She raised her arms and hooked her hands about his neck, pulling his mouth to hers, opening her lips and pushing out her tongue to fence with his.

He began to pant and thrust his penis hard against her. 'Slut,' he hissed through the kiss. 'You crazy slut!'

She drove her leg between his, chafing herself on him, sliding in her nectar, trying to get hard contact for her nub.

He raised his knee and thrust into her crotch and drove his penis up and down her belly. His scrotum rubbed her mons, but she could not come. Now she needed more than rubbing – far more.

She bent her leg up over his thigh, opening herself to him. She pulled herself up his body until his glans nosed between her legs. Then she gasped as she felt the stiffness of his cock pushing to get in her.

Lifting her leg higher, she stretched even more, making herself gape, and working her pelvis to position herself over his cock.

Now he began to flex his hips, driving his penis against her as he whispered, 'This is mad, Jodi.'

'Shut up, Bentonne. Finish what you started in the forest.' She took his mouth again, the kiss sending darts of excitement to the mouth between her legs, working desperately to capture his shaft as he thrust it against her. It pushed between her legs, but she didn't want it there. She wanted it inside her.

Quickly, Jodi manoeuvred him on to his back and rolled on top of him. Now her breasts were squashed against his chest, the vibration of the aircraft transmitting to her nipples.

She dragged herself up him, slipping on his perspiration now. Then she rose, pushing with her hands against his chest, setting her legs astride him. The heat of his shaft between her legs was wonderful. She hadn't realised just how much she had wanted this until the spread lips of her pussy touched his glans. She closed her eyes and swallowed.

He moaned and raised his hips.

Slipping herself over his shaft again, she tried to

make him enter her, but with his hands behind his back, he could not take control.

The hairs of his scrotum tickled at her labia as she moved. Then she rose on her knees, reached under herself and gripped him hard. His cockshaft was slippery with her juice and she almost lost her grip on it. Then as she eased it up and made it nose against her pussy, she moved her knees further apart, stretching herself as widely as she could.

He moaned as he felt her heat. 'Slut,' he whispered. 'You wonderful, horny, wanton slut. I love you.'

He loved her? She shook her head. It was pure lust that he loved. But she didn't care a damn as she sank slowly down. Then she breathed a sigh of satisfaction as she felt him. She had control. She had the smug Mr Bentonne just where she had fantasised about having him for so long, between her legs as she rode him hard.

As the pilot put the plane's nose down sharply, Jodi was thrown forwards, crashing on to Bentonne's chest. Now she could feel his breath, hot on her cheek as it exploded from his lungs. Her lips searched along the smooth skin of his cheek until they found his ear and pushed her tongue into it.

He bit her neck and made her draw a sharp breath.

As their lips met he drove up into her hard, raising her in the air. They both let out a cry of pleasure. She could feel his tension rising under her kiss, and she held there as steadily as she could, her mouth moving sensuously over his, her hips working so her pussy rode his cock in small, tight circles.

He gasped as she pulled herself off him poised to swallow him again. As if on cue the aircraft bumped again, sending the shock wave from his penis deep into her body. She groaned. They were landing and she needed to climax quickly.

As he raised his hips, his penis slipped in deeper. Then the plane jolted and jarred her as it taxied across some grass. Hell, that felt so good – and she was coming.

Now they became quite frantic. They writhed and bucked and twisted. Clearly Bentonne was as intent on getting his climax as she was. As she worked herself over him she felt the head of his penis ripple up inside her sleeve. She felt his pubis jar against her nub. His hairy scrotum tickled at the insides of her thighs. Every little judder of the plane sent wonderful feelings rushing up inside her to fill her belly and swell her breasts.

She leaned right back, forcing her legs apart as widely as she could, slipping on the rubber of the mat. She slid further down his body, forcing his cock right up, making the head of it grind against her G spot. Hell, it was pure bliss as the plane bumped and jarred.

She began to rise and fall, savouring every ripple as the stiff shaft filled her with its girth.

'Geez, what a prick,' she gasped, 'what a prick!'

The small plane halted.

She threw her head back and closed her eyes and drove down one last time. But she could not come.

There were voices by the door.

Jodi rolled off Bentonne just as the compartment was filled with light. She squinted into the glimmer of a rising dawn, half obscured by the blackness of Polder's silhouette. Quickly she tugged up the blanket to cover Bentonne's erection, and glowered at Polders as his great hand grabbed her leg. She kicked out, but she was not quick enough to evade him.

As he dragged her out, the Dutchman's eyes lighted on her nakedness, travelled to her crotch and over her panting belly. He could probably see the wetness of her nectar on her skin and noted that her nipples stood right out.

Jodi glimpsed a hangar, black against the sky, and in the distance, a windmill turning slowly, its white-board cladding rosy in the light of dawn.

She started as a bag was slipped over her head from behind. She turned to cuff her assailant with her tied-up wrists, but he wrapped her in a blanket and whispered lovingly in her ear, 'Don't try to fight me, Jodi. I promise I won't hurt you. I want to make love to you if you'll let me.'

She had forgotten the youth until then. 'Touch me and I'll kill you,' she barked through the sack over her head.

He held her gently around the waist and put his mouth against her cheek. 'I'll suck your tits and kiss your cunt if that's what you like.'

'And I said I'll kill you if you try. Now get off me or I'll knee you.'

He laughed and held her tighter. 'I'll fuck you in any way you want me to. You do need fucking, don't you?' His hand slipped between her legs and felt the slickness of her pussy, as he whispered, 'Yes, I can tell that you do. If you'll let me fuck this, I promise you won't regret it.'

Jodi breathed deeply. It was almost romantic, until Polders growled, 'Leave *dat* alone. She mine!'

Chapter Six

THE SECOND JOURNEY on the floor of a van was uncomfortable. Jodi was wedged between Bentonne and something very hard and cold. With the hood over her eyes she had to use her senses of touch and smell to get a picture of what was going on.

'It was a grass strip,' she whispered to Bentonne, hoping they were alone.

'It didn't take much intelligence to work that out,' he quipped. 'I could feel every little bump.'

'But you enjoyed every bump as well.'

'I endured every one.'

She ignored his change of mood. Did he blame her for not bringing him off? Too bad. 'There was a hangar and I saw a windmill in the distance. I think we're in the Netherlands.'

'There are windmills in southern England too, you know.'

'Not post mills like that one.'

'Quite a detective, aren't you?'

'Yes – I am. Now for Christ's sake tell me what's eating you all of a sudden.'

'Nothing's "eating" me, as you put it. I'm tired.'

'And crabby because you didn't come.'

He snorted. 'If you really want to know, I'm annoyed that I let you get to me again.'

Jodi was incensed, but his attitude would not put her off collecting clues. The slightest scrap of information was valuable to her. She needed to build up as good a mental picture as she could. When she found out where she was she might be able to form a plan for their escape. Then she changed the thought. If Bentonne was going to be annoying again, she would form a plan for her own escape and to hell with him.

She dug him in the ribs. 'At least we haven't woken up at the bottom of the Channel.'

'Don't be so melodramatic, Barens. Even cousin Max wouldn't be so stupid as to think he could get rid of me like that.'

Jodi concentrated on the inside of the van again. An exploration with her foot soon contacted something cold and smooth. Its contents sloshed and bumped when she jogged it. Tracing its outline with her toe, she developed a picture of one of the auxiliary fuel pods off the aircraft. She had glimpsed one just before they'd been bundled into its luggage compartment.

The van started off, chugging along some country track, she guessed. She snuggled up to Bentonne grudgingly for warmth. 'You all right?'

'No, I am not.'

'If you don't stop being so grumpy, I'll elbow you again. Now, have you got any ideas about where they're taking us?'

'I wouldn't tell you if I did have. I still don't trust you in that way.'

Under the hood, Jodi looked in his direction and gave a sigh of exasperation. 'Look – we're in this together. But if you're not going to be cooperative, I'll leave you behind when I find a way out of this hole you've got us into.'

'I didn't get us into any "hole". It was you who brought Maximillian's cretins sniffing around the cottage. Your seduction routine was clearly designed to get me away from there. They've probably stripped it bare by now.'

Jodi ignored him and tried to concentrate on the pieces of the jigsaw that she had, but they were very few.

When the van stopped, cold air flooded in. Then Polders said, 'Come quietly, Mr Bentonne or I hurt *de* woman.' There was a scuffle, then the doors clanged shut. Jodi's spirits sank. Despite her bravado with Bertonne, she felt very alone.

Minutes passed painfully slowly, and she was cold. Although Bentonne had become a pain again, he had at least been warm. Suddenly she was hoisted out of the van and set on her feet. Her neck was clamped by that now-familiar grip. She sniffed hard, trying to discern the difference between Polders's scent and that of the air. The smell of the neighbourhood seemed very familiar, and as her feet were placed on steps going down, she smiled. She was beginning to have a good idea where they might have been brought to. Counting ten cold steps she felt a flat floor. A door creaked open and she was pushed roughly forward.

Jodi blinked as her hood was removed, and found herself looking into the blue eyes of the youth, with Polders just behind him.

The young man grinned and pushed a shock of blond hair from his forehead.

Even though Jodi's pulse began to race as her eyes met his, she held her blanket tightly about her shoulders, stood back and stared him out. She would not be intimidated by any man, let alone a youth.

Polders towered in a low doorway, his cruel eyes scanning Jodi closely. Then he pulled the youth aside, snapping in Dutch, 'She's not for you to play with, Master Hans. I'm going to find your guardian. He'll decide what to do with them. You get off and develop your pictures.' He shambled through the doorway, tugging the youth behind him.

The sound of a heavy bolt being shot concluded the episode. Footsteps resounded sharply down the passage. She noted the direction they went in before another door opened, letting in street noises. Then it slammed. So, the outside door was that way. She added that information to her picture. She blinked, trying to focus in the dimness.

Bentonne lay on a narrow bunk, his hands tied at his sides to the frame. He was covered in a blanket which heaved with his own deep breaths. She stood over him, looking down as he scowled at her.

'If you've come to try to seduce me again and pump me for information, you can forget it, Barens.'

She threw her hair back haughtily and started to explore the room, sniffing at the air. It had a peculiar scent. The ceiling was vaulted, the brickwork was old and crumbling, and a dim bulb hanging from the vault was the only light they had.

Large pipes running through the room kept it very warm. A table sat crookedly on a stone flagged floor, a rickety chair beside it. There were no windows, only a vent in one wall. Jodi smiled. She had been in cellars like this before. The picture was developing in her mind, giving her more and more confidence.

She stood over Bentonne and gestured with her head. 'Nice place. Period decor. I must say your family have good taste. First a dingy cottage and now a filthy cellar.'

'Being catty won't help our situation, Barens.'

Jodi narrowed her eyes. 'And being bad tempered with me just because you're not getting your own way for once won't help us either.'

'No, but untying me would.'

Aware of her pubis, which was visible to him through the blanket, she pulled the covering around her as she shook her head. 'I can't untie you.'

'You mean you won't.'

She shrugged. 'They've used plastic ties. They'll have to be cut off. Anyway, in your present mood, I wouldn't release you even if I could.'

They lapsed into silence as she hunched up on the bunk beside him. Then she dozed.

Waking with a start as Bentonne stretched, Jodi scanned the room. Nobody had entered, but her acute hearing picked up the sound of breathing coming through the door grille. She caught a glimpse of the youth's eyes looking through the bars. Ignoring him, she rose and began to explore the room again. Checking to see that the blue eyes were still watching, she awkwardly fetched the chair and stood up by the vent, dropping the blanket in the process. She knew that both the watcher and Bentonne would be looking at her nakedness. She even opened her legs slightly, feeling herself moisten as she did so. It was crazy, but the danger of her situation – being shut up with one man tied to a bed and another watching her clandestinely – was arousing her again. Knowing that the youth had already watched Bentonne fucking her at the cottage, and had been really horny at the airfield, she decided to play his game.

Jodi tried to take her attention from the tingling between her legs and sniffed at the vent. She looked down on Bentonne and was about to tell him that she smelled a canal when she stopped herself. It was best that the amorous young Dutchman watching at the door did not suspect she knew too much.

So she sat on the edge of the bunk, and leaned over Bentonne, smiling, her face directly above his.

He turned away as she went to kiss him lightly. At the same time she whispered, 'I smelled a canal. I thought I recognised it when I got out of the van. I'm pretty sure we're in one of the old spice warehouses in Amsterdam.'

'Of course we're in Amsterdam,' he hissed derisively.

She sniffed. 'From that I deduce that your cousin has a place in Amsterdam.'

'Don't pretend you didn't know that, Jodi.'

She ignored his mood and kissed him again, making him turn his head away. 'My god you're such a bastard, Bentonne.'

She sat by him for some minutes as she worked out a plan of escape. He wouldn't like it, but that was too bad. A thrill went through her as she walked her fingers up his thigh.

He tried to move but could not. 'You can stop that, you slut. You won't seduce me again.'

'I'm not trying to seduce you, Bentonne. I've got a plan to escape from here. All you have to do is lie back and think of England.'

He scanned her face. 'What witchery are you up to now?'

'Protest all you like, but it won't do you any good.' She stripped the blanket down to leave him bare. Hell, she was behaving like the slut he thought her to be, but she was loving every minute of it. And the knowledge of being watched as she stripped the man was adding to her tension.

Bentonne glowered as she lifted his limp organ and

81

tried to make it swell. This time it did not respond as she ran his foreskin gently up and down.

'Stop it, Jodi,' he snapped.

'Lie still, won't you?' she whispered, and took his glans between her lips and sucked.

He groaned, 'I said, stop it, Jodi!'

'Look,' She took her mouth reluctantly from him, 'If you want to get out of here, you'd better start cooperating with me.'

A silence hung in the air as they weighed each other up, each trying to guess what the other was thinking.

Jodi steeled herself. If she was going to get herself out of this mess, she must not turn soft. The feel of him between her fingers was getting to her again. When she was wound up like this, she could not focus on anything else but getting her fulfilment. But sex had got her into the mess and might get her out again.

She sucked at him again, feeling him swell slightly to the heat inside her mouth. It took her some more minutes before she had him hard enough to enter her when she was ready. All the time, the watcher at the door looked on with fascination.

Jodi knelt astride Bentonne's legs and as she bent to take his penis in her mouth again, she showed her bottom to the watcher. Could he see how swollen the plump lips of her pussy were? Could he see how moist?

Jodi felt herself stretch as she widened her knees. Now she was open, she could sense a cool breeze coming from the door, fanning between her legs and cooling her labia. As the door creaked open, then closed, she felt the most erotic sensations she had ever had. Then she heard deep breathing in the room.

As she bent to take Bentonne's penis deep into her throat, her breasts hung fully, their surfaces tingling as they dragged on his legs. Then she moved to straddle his hips, put her hands between her legs and pulled his cock sharply upwards. With a little spring on her knees she rose then she sank down on it, gasping at the wonderful sensation as it filled and widened her until she felt her nubbin on his pubis.

As she heard a movement at the door, her heart beat like a drum and she began to rise and fall, wiggling her hips to feel Bentonne's cock deep inside her sleeve. She did not turn, but continued to moan as she wriggled on her prize. Then suddenly she pretended to catch sight of the youth watching her intently.

Throwing her head back she let out a laugh and was just about to call out to him in Dutch when she bit her lip. They didn't know that she spoke their language and that might be the biggest advantage that she had.

As she beckoned the youth with her head to come to her, he was already unfastening his belt.

Jodi thought that her heart would stop. It was the biggest risk she had taken in this game. It was far more dangerous than being caught by Bentonne in the forest.

Quickly, she rose and watched Bentonne's shaft slip from her, fully hard and shining with her juice. Then she stood absolutely naked before the surprised young man, her breasts pushed out and her legs apart, watching as he slipped his zip and dropped his jeans to reveal the pouch that contained his straining cock.

Chapter Seven

JODI SMILED AT the young Dutchman as he scanned her body excitedly.

'So you want to fuck me, do you?' she whispered. 'But I'm not sure you're man enough for me – I don't do boys.' She saw a flash of anger in his eyes as she said, 'But if your prick's bigger than this, I might give you a try.' She lifted Bentonne's cock and worked the foreskin, then let it go derisively.

As he kicked his trousers off and stripped his shirt, Jodi swallowed hard. He was firm and trim – and sexy. She wanted already to lay him down and explore him with her mouth. With his eyes on the full forms of her breasts, she pushed her nipples out and pouted seductively as she whispered, 'Show me your prick.'

He smirked confidently, fingering his bulge as she took a step towards him, her labia throbbing hard. Then, as he focused on her hardened nipples, his tongue tip licking his lips, Jodi stretched out her tied hands and felt his hardness through his briefs. She slipped her fingers into them and pushed them slowly down. Kneeling, she watched his long and slender penis as it emerged, already so stiff that the head was deep purple and the veins were pumping hard. She put her lips to it and kissed, breathing in that scent which always bred in her a demand to be fucked.

'What's your name?' she whispered, working at his foreskin, fingering the web to make him jerk.

'My name is Hans.'

'And how big can you make this, Hans?' she asked as he pushed his shaft into her mouth, just as he had watched Bentonne do to her.

He looked at Bentonne on the bunk and smirked with triumph as Jodi ran her tongue around his glans. She was wet with the strange excitement of the danger coursing through her as she rose and kissed him lightly on the navel. Then she pulled his nipples one by one and ran a line of kisses up his strong, young neck until she reached his mouth. Trembling now as he neared the point where he was hers, she put her lips to his and took his cock, whispering, 'Show me how you use this.'

He took her around the neck and pulled her mouth to his and slipped the other hand between her legs. She felt him tense, as one finger explored the slickness of her furrow. His fingers working on her smooth and supple skin made her tremble. He was so delightful, even if naive, and she wanted to pet him and fondle him and lick his balls to make him fuck her hard. But she steeled herself to keep to her resolve. If she was to escape, this might be her only chance. All she had to do was raise her knee sharply, and he would writhe in agony at her feet. But he was too beautiful to hurt, even though she was desperate to flee. Instead, she pushed him hard so he reeled across the room, crashing into the wall and sinking winded to the floor, his penis wagging widely.

Jodi quickly searched his pockets but could not find a knife to cut Bentonne's bonds. She looked at Bentonne with resignation in her eyes. She had no time to stop now and release him.

Hans was already rising to his feet, his eyes filled with hurt. Jodi backed towards the door as he launched himself at her. She raised her leg and gave him a karate kick on the chest which sent him down again. Spread-eagled on his back, his penis was rock hard, his testes drawn up close beneath its shaft.

While she tried to open the heavy door, desperately tugging at the handle, Hans sprang up and caught her around the waist. They crashed to the floor as she tried to twist away, his penis hard against the crevice of her bottom.

She attempted to elbow him but he had her fast, one strong young arm around her waist, one hand upon her breast. He curled his legs about her thighs and spread her legs apart.

Slick with sweat from the heated room and the effort of the fight, Jodi slipped and could not get away.

'Give in,' he whispered in her ear. 'Give in and I will not hurt you, even though you tried to hurt me.'

She rolled, but he was tenacious. Now he had her flat on her belly, her breasts squashed against the floor, her arms out in front of her, still tied at the wrists.

'Give in,' he rasped.

'Get off,' She spat as she reached for the leg of Bentonne's bunk to pull herself up.

The heat of his body on her back contrasted with the coldness of the stone. But the most curious thing of all was that as she felt the head of his penis pushing at her cleft, she wanted it there. Something perverse in her always seemed to succumb to a powerful man, and this youth was not only wonderfully virile, but powerful as well.

He opened her legs and drove his cock inside her, biting her neck as he began to fuck her hard. 'Give in. You cannot win, Jodi. I am far stronger than you.'

Despite her need to feel him, she writhed, managed to unbalance him and was on her feet in a trice.

They circled, half bending, each with fingers clawed. His eyes were sparkling with elation and hers with sheer excitement. She had completely forgotten Bentonne as he struggled with his bonds. All she was aware of now was the long and slender penis erupting from a pelt of golden hair as Hans closed in on her.

Their fingers locked.

She twisted and got away.

He circled again, his eyes intent on hers, full of confidence. He seemed to think that she was his, as he licked his lips and lunged.

But she caught his little finger and twisted it, sending him to his knees. He knelt, looking up at her for mercy, she could have broken it easily. She could have kicked him in the crotch; his balls hung freely now beneath that rigid cock. Or she could have smashed him in the mouth with her fist. Why wasn't he ugly and repulsive like that monster, Polders?

Jodi pushed the youth aside, shot out of the room and bolted the door. As she peered through the grille, Hans gave her a look of desperation.

Bentonne looked like thunder when he saw what she had done. But she could not stop now. He would have to take his chances. If she could escape, she might come back for him. If not . . . She stopped the thought. There was no point in being negative.

Jodi reached the outer door but found it firmly locked. She turned on her heels, searching for another way. A staircase leading upward was the only route from there. She sprinted up with long-legged strides, her breasts bouncing painfully as she went. The nipples were set hard; her belly felt so tight. Her breathing rasped for all the world to hear as she reached a corridor above and rested for some seconds.

At one end of the passage stood a single door. She chose to go for that. Logically it should lead to kitchens or servants' quarters.

This corridor was plush, with carved and inlaid doors marching down its length. At an ornate table with letters and a newspaper she stopped. Snatching up the paper, she held it to her pubis. It was an instinctive gesture and really quite futile, since she could not cover her nudity entirely.

As she tiptoed over polished floorboards, there came a shout from behind her. She hurried faster, frightened in case her steps be heard. Then a door halfway down the corridor swung open.

Her reaction was to dart inside the nearest room. With her hands still tied, she closed the door with difficulty and stood stock still, her back to its cold surface, her belly pumping hard.

Jodi's photographer's mind snapped the room in a fraction of a second. Ornate ceilings met her gaze, gilded and painted with pink-cheeked cherubs floating above nearly naked women bathing at a pool. A huge, oak desk, richly upholstered couches, and chairs with carved wood backs stood sedately on a Persian carpet. A computer terminal occupied one corner. Large windows revealed the unmistakable stepped gables of mediaeval houses lining the inner canals of Amsterdam.

Then heavy, running steps and loud shouting in coarse Dutch made her freeze.

'What's the matter, Polders?'

'The woman got away, *Mijnheer*.'

'She what?'

'She tricked the boy.'

'You fool! You should never have let him go down there.'

'I'm sorry sir. I forbade him to . . .'

'Don't stand there making excuses for yourself, cheesehead. Get him to help you find her. I'll deal with you both later.'

Someone ran past Jodi's door. The steps were heavy and she guessed that they were Polders's. Then lighter steps came past her door, but stopped.

'Polders!' someone shouted. 'Come back here – I think I've found the girl.'

Jodi's heart missed a beat. To her horror, the door handle turned, scraping at the bare skin of her flank.

Next to her stood a large, double-fronted cupboard, one panelled door ajar. It was her only hope. But as she darted into it, her newspaper tore and floated to the floor. She had caught it in the outer door as she had shut it, and probably left it as a clue for searching eyes.

Inside the musty cupboard, she struggled to hold her breath.

When sunlight flooded in on her, she tried to focus through it. All she could make out was the figure of a man. Behind him in a haze of light, the unmistakable silhouette of Polders loomed.

She sank down to the floor just as she had sunk among the tree roots in the forest. And just as Bertonne had stood above her, his legs apart, his broad hands on his hip bones, this man stood now, except that he was fully dressed.

'Well, what have we here? A naked maiden in my wardrobe? It must be my lucky day.' The voice was soft and cultured. Although there was the slightest hint of a Dutch accent, his English was clear and faultless.

'Don't touch me!' she protested.

He lifted his hands in mock self-defence. 'All right. But promise that you won't attack me,' he laughed. It was a free, light laugh, and one that contrasted sharply with the shouting in the corridor.

'All right, Polders, you can go,' he said in cultured Dutch. 'I'll ring for you if I need your help. But I trust that I can handle this young woman better than you have.' Jodi was aware of Polders's scowl as he slunk out and shut the door. She turned her gaze on the other man; her eyes adjusted to the glare.

'Come out, Jodi,' he said softly. 'I promise I won't hurt you.'

She rose, her fears allayed by the kindness in his voice. Still clutching her paper, she stood and faced him squarely. As she focused on his face, she took an involuntary breath.

It was as if she was standing before Dean Bentonne, apart from the blondness of his hair and the blueness of his eyes. The features of his face were almost identical to Dean's, a duplicate of the same broad mouth she'd liked so much, smiling at her now. The eyes were deep and clear, his posture self-assured. He was every inch a businessman in a light-blue, double-breasted suit. A clear complexion and a devastating smile, with lips that curled at the corners made her apprehension melt away.

He found a pair of scissors and cut Jodi's wrist straps in a trice; she rubbed her wrists to get the circulation back.

'Here,' he said, 'take this,' and handed her his jacket. 'Come and sit down. I'll order you some coffee. And would you like some breakfast?'

Jodi hadn't realised just how hungry she was until he mentioned food. As he keyed an intercom and ordered breakfast, she looked at a gilded carriage-clock sitting on the desk. It was more than twelve hours since she'd eaten stew with Bentonne at the cottage.

'I'm Maximillian Van de Rohe, by the way,' he crooned.

She could not check her surprise. 'Van de Rohe? But I thought you were a Bentonne.'

He shook his head. 'No, I come from a branch of the family on Dean Bentonne's mother's side. But enough of the family tree. Let's talk about you, Miss Barens.'

'How do you know my name?'

He smiled. 'Surely you realise that it was I who hired you to track my cousin to that cottage in the woods? He disappeared some weeks ago and we were very anxious to find him.'

She snorted. 'I bet you were.'

Their eyes met briefly before she glanced away, feeling a flush rise to her cheeks.

As he pulled the jacket close around her, his thumbs just brushed her nipples. She couldn't tell if it was planned or not. When she looked into his eyes again, there was no sign of lechery there, nor the kind of lust that Polders's eyes had betrayed.

As Max led her gently to a leather chair set before the desk, she was acutely aware that her pubis showed beneath the soft blue worsted of the jacket. So what? She had been stripped and ogled and photographed having sex with Bentonne, and was past caring about her nudity. Even if she were dressed, this man would probably take her to some bedroom, strip her and have her whenever it pleased him. In a way it would be a relief. If he was anything like Dean Bentonne, it might be pleasant. It might even be exciting.

'I hear you've had quite an adventure,' he said as he studied her.

'That's putting it mildly.' She threw her head back with annoyance.

'I really am sorry, Jodi. That fellow Polders is such a

91

bungler. He was sent to keep an eye on Dean after you had located him, not to abduct you both. I hope you will let me try to make amends to you.'

As she glowered and tried to rise, the jacket came open and bared her breasts. She tugged it angrily together, and tried to cool her temper. This man was a cool operator, and he seemed not to be beating about the bush. He seemed to assume that Bentonne had filled her in with his background details.

'I guessed you were behind it,' she said, throwing her hair back haughtily. 'But l haven't got any pictures for you. I suppose you'll want your money back.'

Van de Rohe gave her a scomful look. 'No, I don't want any money back.' He opened an inlaid box on the desk and took out a packet of prints. Thumbing through them slowly, he smiled wistfully.

Unable to contain her anger, Jodi snatched the prints from him, dropping some on the desk. As they both stared down, the full realisation of how she'd been duped with Bentonne struck her with some force. Hans must have been in the woods all the time, taking photographs of her.

The first shot showed Bentonne standing naked before the oak tree. The strong, yellow light behind him threw his profile into silhouette. His torso was taut as he thrust his pelvis forward, his fully rampant penis erupting in a curve. The eyes of the young, blond woman cowering beneath him were rooted on it. Her expression was one of wonder, not of fear.

The next shot was a close-up of Bentonne standing over the young woman, his testicles hanging heavily, raindrops running off them. Bright sunlight lit a bead of rain poised at the very tip of the straining shaft.

Jodi swallowed hard at the next shot showing her near-nakedness. She was pushing down her shorts to bare herself to the man. In the next shot he had her against the tree, her legs around his hips as she tried to rub herself on him. The expression of great need written on her face was frozen in that instant for anyone to see.

She shot Max a withering look.

'I'm afraid that my protégé, Hans, got a bit carried away,' Maximillian said softly. 'But I think the pictures are rather good. Hans is already a master of photography, wouldn't you agree?'

Under normal circumstances Jodi would have agreed. The photographs were technically superb.

'I've seen better,' she snorted.

'Better than these?' Max asked, fanning more photos on the desk.

Now Jodi saw the scene before the fire. She saw herself lying there naked with Bentonne, his leg between her own, one hand on her breast, the nipple poking out between his fingers.

Jodi pushed a print away across the desk. The photographer had used a fast film. He had probably only resorted to flash to get their attention at the end, to draw them out of the cottage so it could be searched.

The next sequence showed her licking Bentonne's penis, which was shining with spit in the firelight. Then came a shot where he had turned the tables on her. It was somewhat blurred as he covered her. The camera had caught her vulva stretched widely as he pinned her down and pushed her legs right back. Her nipples stood so proudly against the firelight. Looking at the photographs was turning Jodi on. Was Van de Rohe showing them to her to stimulate her, or to annoy her? Did he think that she would get so hot he'd find her easy?

She tried to still the excitement running through her body. She shifted her position on the chair.

'And these last four are the most revealing, I believe,' he said holding up a print.

Jodi took a long breath. The shot showed her on her knees in front of Bentonne. He had assumed the same stance as he had done in the forest, his hands on his hips, his penis standing stiff. But this time she had her mouth over the tip. Her eyes were closed as she clearly savoured it. This time, instead of little raindrops, the saliva from her mouth trickled down his shaft, which reflected pinkness from the hot coals of the fire. The fine hairs of the man's brown legs contrasted well against her skin as her breasts were moulded to his contours.

The second of the final four showed Jodi with her eyes closed, her hands clawing at his thighs. He held his head right back and thrust his cock in hard. His eyes were closed in ecstasy and his mouth gasped at the sensation she created with her tongue.

Van de Rohe handed her the last two prints, saying, 'I'm afraid these two are rather overexposed. Hans must have turned his flash on by mistake.'

The penultimate shot made Jodi close her eyes for a second. She had forgotten that he'd come. There was a look of relief on Bentonne's face as a long, thick jet of semen shot into the air. Caught by the flash it hung there, as Jodi looked towards the camera.

The final shot was indeed overexposed. But this somehow highlighted the horror on the faces of the naked man and woman by the fire, thick fluid running down her neck and surging from his glans.

Jodi shoved the prints at Van de Rohe and turned away. In one way she was furious, in another she was aroused. She closed her eyes, trying to push away the images, but they would not go. Her breasts were swollen; her nipples hurt. Her vulva sucked upon the leather of the chair. Her heart beat like a jungle drum and, to cap it all, a clone of Bentonne was seated close beside her, studying her breasts as they welled out from his jacket.

She pulled the jacket to again. 'Nobody will publish those,' she snapped. 'You'll never sell them.'

He shook his head slowly. 'I do not intend to sell them, Jodi.'

She was surprised. 'So why go to all that trouble to get them?'

He smiled. 'Let's just say that Hans became rather over-zealous in his mission. But now I shall keep them as an insurance policy for the future.'

'Blackmail, you mean.'

He shook his head. 'A bit of leverage, perhaps. The Board of Directors of Bentonne Universal are rather old-fashioned, I'm afraid. They expect their executives to show the highest standards of morality.' He laughed.

'And you plan to show them these pictures so they won't appoint Dean as Chief Exec instead of you.'

He frowned playfully. 'I hope that won't be necessary. After you had left – so hurriedly – my agents found evidence in that cottage to show that my cousin has been milking the company of millions.'

'*He's* been milking your company?'

'Apparently so. He has been hacking into the computers of our various subsidiaries, and moving funds into his own accounts.'

'But that's no excuse for kidnapping him.'

Van de Rohe shrugged. 'I have to make sure that he isn't at liberty to go off somewhere else and do the same thing. The Board meets this week to consider what we should do with him.'

'But shouldn't you tell the police?'

He smiled thinly. 'Family firms are rather protective when it comes to black sheep, Jodi. We would rather keep this little matter discreet. I'm sure you understand.'

'And you think I'll blab it out.'

He shrugged. 'I hope that now you know the truth, you will see the matter my way.'

Jodi was in a spin. This whole thing had turned on its head. Bentonne's so-called surveillance operation from his attic had really been a cover for his greedy purposes. But that didn't excuse Van de Rohe's treatment of her.

As she looked into his smiling eyes, she blurted, 'I think this whole thing stinks. And you had no right to kidnap me.'

'Quite so. That was a silly thing to do. But as I said before, I hope you'll let me make amends for Polders's stupidity in dragging you back here.'

'I doubt you can do that. Abduction is a serious business, Mr Van de Rohe.'

'So is divulging you client's affairs, Miss Barens. Your contract on this job specifically forbids you to do so, on pain of prosecution. I could have you jailed for years.'

She rose and faced him, her nakedness uncovered as she pushed the jacket back to plant her hands upon her hips. 'You sod!' Her breasts shook as she said it, and her belly pumped with anger, but she didn't care a damn.

The glint in his eyes unnerved her. 'It was a normal business arrangement, Miss Barens,' he said softly. 'And I hope that the bonus you were promised on completion of the surveillance job will recompense you entirely for the subsequent inconvenience you have suffered.'

Jodi sank back in the chair. She had forgotten the huge bonus in her contract. It had seemed unreal that any simple surveillance job would be worth that much bonus on completion. Now she understood how skilfully she had been manipulated.

She clamped her arms across her breasts. 'I don't

understand why you had to go to those elaborate antics to kidnap Bentonne. Polders could have simply walked in with a gun.'

Van de Rohe nodded. 'Quite so. But I told you, Polders bungled the whole thing. His only instructions were to find out where my cousin was running his clandestine operation from and to search the premises if he could without arousing suspicion. Apart from leading my men to Dean, you were a diversion which I hoped would take his mind off his operation for long enough to lower his guard.'

'You could have sent a prostitute for that.'

'He wouldn't have been taken in by such a woman, Jodi, even if she could have tracked him down. No – I needed a well-educated, intelligent, stunningly attractive, sexually provocative young woman with ability in tracking, as well as a deep sense of justice. You were the ideal candidate.'

Jodi didn't know if she was supposed to feel flattered or not. Secretly she felt quite proud of those attributes. But they had led her into this mess, and she would have to apply them now to get herself out of it again.

She scowled. 'I think it was a mean trick to use me like that.'

He brushed her hair back from her forehead. 'Of course. But there is a lot at stake here, Jodi. Many little people will lose their livelihoods if my cousin's greedy actions close their businesses.'

That struck a note of empathy in Jodi. The welfare of such people and the way they were treated by big companies like Bentonne Universal had been one of her motivations for taking the assignment to tail Bentonne. Had she not declared her intention to take the man down a peg or two?

'All right.' She looked up at Van de Rohe hard. 'I'm

sorry I was rude to you. But I still think it was rotten of Hans to take such pictures of Bentonne and me. I could prosecute him for invasion of our privacy.'

Van de Rohe smiled wryly as he took another packet from the box.

Chapter Eight

JODI CLOSED HER eyes as Van de Rohe fanned another set of prints. They were her photos, taken as she'd spied on Bentonne by the forest pool. His men must have found the film in her bag before Bentonne had taken it in and burned the blank film from her camera.

Jodi glanced at her shot of Bentonne as he bent to exercise, his testicles swinging. When he had stood and half turned, she had zoomed in on his penis arcing out from his belly as he'd pushed his pelvis out. The shot had even caught the hairs of his scrotum, shining in the stormy light. The tight skin of his torso was slick as it bulged to show the muscles of a perfect body.

Van de Rohe smiled. 'Not bad, are they? You and Hans have much in common, I think. Perhaps you should get together some time.'

He clearly did not know that she and the youth had 'got together' already.

'I think I'll keep these safe until our business is closed,' he said softly as he put the prints in the box, locking it pointedly. Then he flicked through Hans's pictures again, stopping at one where Jodi had licked Bentonne slowly between his legs.

'If you think I'm going to do that with you, you can forget it,' Jodi snapped.

Max raised his hands defensively and gave a playful smile. 'Nothing could have been further from my thoughts.'

She was just about to call him a liar when a knock came at the door. She spun around as Max called, 'Come in.'

Jodi was surprised: instead of the ugly Polders, the bearer of a breakfast tray was a stunningly beautiful young woman.

'Bring it here, Safronne, thank you,' Van de Rohe said softly.

The girl looked at him with admiration in her eyes. They were large, black eyes, slanting gently upward. Her oval face and the smooth, honey tone of her skin told Jodi that she was probably Indonesian.

The girl set the tray of coffee and fresh croissants on the desk, bowed slightly to Van de Rohe and backed away. As she reached the door, Van de Rohe called out, 'Have a room prepared for Miss Barens, Safronne, please. She'll probably be staying with us for a few days.'

Jodi looked up at him sharply. 'So – you intend to keep me a prisoner.'

He shrugged. 'That depends upon you. If you try to leave, I shall have to cancel your bonus.'

'But that's coercion!'

'It is business, my love. But, regardless of that, I'd very much like you to stay. It could be pleasant if you choose to make it so. White or black?' he asked as he poured a cup of coffee and set it on the desk for her. Then he offered her a croissant. Yellow butter and rich, plum jam made her mouth water. What the hell, she thought, she must eat to get her strength up no matter what he planned. As she munched the croissant, he watched her intently.

'You seem nervous of me, Jodi. I wonder what lies that cousin of mine has told you about me.'

She shrugged, still unwilling to trust him completely.

'Did he tell you that I'm a womaniser of the worst sort, or some kind of wicked monster out to wrest his birthright from him?'

She nodded between bites. 'Something like that.'

Van de Rohe laughed lightly. 'I might have guessed. Dean has always had a vivid imagination.' He leaned close and whispered, 'Between you and me, Jodi, I think he's rather paranoid.'

She looked at him askance. 'But how do I know which of you is telling the truth?'

His eyes narrowed momentarily.

She wished she hadn't said it. As her client, offering a large bonus, he was due more allegiance than Bentonne.

Van de Rohe sipped a cup of coffee, not taking his eyes off her face. 'You really liked him, didn't you?'

She shrugged.

'Women have always melted under that charm of his. But underneath, there is a cool and calculating man, Jodi.'

She nodded. She could relate to that.

Van de Rohe poured more coffee and continued. 'Dean has always been a shifty one. And ever since we were young, he's vied with me to be top dog. It riles him to think that I might be elected Chief Executive instead of him. He's never acknowledged that I am more successful than he is.'

It was said with such calmness and lack of malice that it impressed Jodi. Bentonne had been far more passionate in his remarks about his cousin.

101

Van de Rohe fingered the photo of Jodi on her back with her legs spread widely. She was distracted as his thumb stroked the image as if he were fantasising about stroking the real, soft flesh between her legs. Then he said almost wistfully, 'Dean was always jealous of me. He had plenty of women, but he always wanted mine.' He smiled as he picked up the print of her under the oak tree with her legs about Bentonne's waist, the curve of Bentonne's shaft nudging into her pussy. Looking at it again, she vividly recalled the sensation as it eased her open and slipped inside.

'You are very beautiful, Jodi, and very provocative.'

Here it comes, she said to herself. He's making his move.

'Am I?' she snapped.

'Yes, you are.' He touched her cheek gently and then withdrew. Much to her surprise, she found she liked his touch, but she was damned if she was going to let him know that.

Max picked up a print of Bentonne fucking her hard in front of the fire; she could recall those thrusts quite strongly.

He fanned the prints again. 'I knew that my cousin would find you too alluring to resist.'

'Really.'

'And I guessed that he would pursue my men when he found that you had led them to his hideout. He's a very secretive fellow, and wary of being photographed with women.'

When Jodi looked up into the Dutchman's eyes, she thought she saw a hint of jealousy there as he ran a finger down her flank on another of the prints.

She finished her croissant and sat back abruptly. 'Thanks for the breakfast. Now – am I supposed to lie back on the couch and open my legs for you?'

He pretended to be shocked, but she could see a glint of interest in his clear, blue eyes. 'Really, Jodi, you do seem to have a very colourful imagination – and a prodigious need for making love.'

'Isn't that what you want?'

He shook his head. 'What I want is for you be my guest and relax.'

'For how long?'

He smiled. 'For two or three days. By that time I will have finished my investigation into Dean's treachery and reported to the Board. When they have decided what action to take against him, and have appointed a new Chief Executive, I shall give you your bonus cheque and you will be free to go. I'll fly you back to England if you like.'

She shrugged. 'OK. It sounds like a good deal.'

'Good. But you must agree not to try to leave the house; not even to go outside the doors. You will forfeit your bonus if you do.'

She nodded. 'All right. I agree.'

'Excellent. I'm sure you will enjoy yourself. I'm planning a wonderful party for tomorrow night.'

She smiled, feeling able to relax at last. 'Sounds interesting. But do you expect me to come dressed like this?' She stood before him, the jacket open, naked for him to view. Like Bentonne, he was a big man, strongly built and athletic. His skin was clear and sun-browned, his teeth perfect. When he reached forward to close her jacket, as if he were embarrassed by her nudity, she saw that his hands were smooth, the fingers long and immaculately manicured. As he held the jacket together, she caught a whiff of aftershave which sent her senses reeling.

'I shall call Safronne to show you to your room. She will take care of you. Just ask her for anything you need.

She will find you something that will make the most of your beauty. She is most adept at bringing out the best in beautiful women.' He lifted her hair and let it fall. 'I'll see you later then. Eight o'clock for dinner, shall we say?'

Jodi felt herself melting. It had been like that with Bentonne too. What was it about such men that dissolved her caution and made her want them so?

Maximillian pushed the intercom and summoned the Asian girl. The silence between them was quite poignant while they waited. He sat again on the edge of his desk, filing through the photos as casually as if they were family snaps.

Jodi swallowed hard as she saw the images of her naked body pass through his hands. She was sure he stopped at those of the rampant Bentonne just a little longer than her own. Was he gay? Surely not. He looked so masculine. There wasn't the slightest hint of effeminacy about him.

When Safronne came she smiled at Jodi sweetly. As they turned to leave, Maximillian took his jacket from her shoulders. It surprised Jodi that he would leave her naked. Snatching up the newspaper, she put it to her breasts for a moment. Then she relented and lowered it, holding up her head with pride. After he had run his eyes down from her breasts to her pubis and back with evident admiration, he turned away.

'Thanks for breakfast, Mr Van de Rohe,' she called from the door.

He waved her an acknowledgement. 'You're welcome, Jodi. And, please call me Max. My friends do.'

Safronne bowed as she closed the door. Taking Jodi by the hand, she led her through the rambling house. Winding stairs spiralled upward and flattened out at another passage. Soon they stopped before a large oak door.

Safronne ushered Jodi in, smiled and gestured around the spacious room. 'This is my room, but you are welcome to share it while you stay. All the other bedrooms are taken for the party tomorrow night. If you want to bathe now and rest, I shall bring you some new garments. If there is anything you want at all, just ask me.' She bowed slightly and smiled.

Jodi nearly bowed back but stopped herself. 'Thanks. I think I'll sleep before I do anything else. I'm almost dead on my feet.'

It was only when Safronne had left that Jodi really took note of the room, which was high and airy. Panelled in richly polished wood with a moulded plaster ceiling, it had an air of opulence. The oak floor was uneven, the planks worn smooth by several hundred years of well-heeled feet. A large bed dominated the space, and a set of mirrors looked down from its embroidered canopy.

Heavy red curtains hung at tall windows which showed the quadrangle of a yard. There was no escape from here, even if she had needed one.

She wandered around the room, studying oriental silk pictures on the walls, the pungency of incense in the air, and the tinkle of little tubular bells hanging from the canopy of the bed. These all witnessed that this was indeed the room of the Asian girl.

Jodi ventured into a modern bathroom, but she was too tired to bathe. She needed sleep. She needed to renew her energies and be ready for anything that threatened.

She stood in the centre of the room, still clutching the remnants of the newspaper. She looked at it and smiled. Rubbing a thumb over the heading, she made prints in several places. Then she folded the paper carefully, knelt, and slipped it under the bed, pushing it up into the springing. She rubbed her hands together, her task well-done, and sank down on the bed feeling very alone. Lying back, she pulled the duvet over herself, curled up in a ball and closed her eyes.

A sound beside the bed brought Jodi to full alert. She shot up and rubbed her eyes, not knowing quite how long she'd slept. Her gaze was met by the most arresting eyes she'd ever seen. As black as jet, yet clear as crystal, they belonged to the graceful, smooth-skinned Safronne.

Jodi caught her breath. There seemed to be electricity flowing between them as Safronne's gaze took hold of hers and held it fast. Jodi felt as if her inner world were being tapped and examined very closely. She coughed nervously and turned away for a second. When she turned back again, Safronne smiled with clear amusement.

'Good afternoon, miss,' the silky voice whispered. 'I have brought you some lunch.'

'What time is it?' Jodi rubbed her eyes hard and took several deep breaths as she tried to focus on her visitor. Tall and slender, in a garment of shimmering silk she stood at the bedside with a silver tray, more beautiful than Jodi had realised.

Jodi was surprised when her pulse began to quicken and as she sat up to face the girl, she tried to still it.

'The time is three o'clock,' Safronne smiled. 'Would you like to eat?' She sat close to Jodi on the edge of the bed and placed the tray between them. Then she took a grape and held it to Jodi's lips.

Jodi let it in and closed her mouth.

Another grape was followed by a strawberry dipped in cream and the finest castor sugar, which left a creamy line around her mouth. To Jodi's surprise the Asian girl reached out and ran her finger around her creamy lips. Then she took her finger to her own lips and sucked it very slowly.

Jodi's pulse was racing as the black eyes searched her own. Were they trying to divine the effect this intimate feast was having?

When Safronne took a banana and peeled it very slowly, Jodi's interest grew. She watched intently as the girl dipped the banana into sugar and sucked on it as if it were a phallus, while all the time her gaze did not leave Jodi's eyes.

Safronne took another banana and pushed it into Jodi's mouth; it reminded her of the sensation of having Bentonne's shaft there.

Jodi closed her eyes as she sucked on the banana. When she felt a slight warmth on her breast, she opened them again. Looking down, she found the beguiling finger stroking at one nipple. She hadn't given her nakedness a second thought until that moment. It had seemed perfectly natural to sit with her breasts quite bare.

When Safronne dipped her finger into the jug of cream and spread a ring around one rampant nipple, Jodi began to shake. When the honey-brown fingers took a pinch of sugar to sprinkle on the cream, Jodi could not stop her inner thighs from trembling so violently she thought that it would show beneath the duvet.

But Safronne took no notice. Instead, she took Jodi by the shoulders and eased her back into the pillows. Then she took the sugar-coated nipple between her lips and sucked, tantalisingly slowly.

The place between Jodi's legs was hot and throbbing now. She could feel her pussy swelling nicely. The nipple grew and, not to be outdone, the other hardened with it. Jodi's vaginal walls seemed to flutter with every little tug of the highly bowed lips.

Just as suddenly as Safronne had begun her seduction, she stopped and sat back smiling.

'I have brought you some clothes.' It was said so matter-of-factly, with no hint of romance, that Jodi wondered if she had imagined that the girl had just removed her lips from sucking both her nipples.

'Thanks for the clothes. That was very kind of you.'

Safronne's smile flashed again and her eyes lit with pleasure as Jodi looked at a shimmering garment on the bed.

Jodi couldn't stop herself from smiling at the girl. She knew her face was flushed. Did the light in her eyes show how much she'd liked the gentle suckling of her breasts?

Safronne crooned, 'You're welcome,' and brushed Jodi's cheek with the backs of slender fingers. Then she peeled back the duvet to bare Jodi completely and examined her unashamedly. Jodi felt admired, not violated by the slanting eyes. When Safronne reached out and touched the blond hair of her pubis, Jodi almost recoiled – but she stopped herself in time. It was not a lascivious touch but one of curiosity. Was the Asian girl amused at the mat of golden hair that covered the triangle of her mons and curled between her legs?

Safronne went to the bathroom; Jodi heard the water run. She felt demure as she stood at the bathroom door, and when Safronne smiled sweetly and crooked her forefinger, she felt drawn to the girl as well as to the bath. Already naked, Jodi knew there was no awkward undressing to be done. Safronne held out a slender hand, and Jodi took it and stepped as elegantly as she could into the steaming water.

The herby scent that wafted to her nose and the

vibrant heat brought memories of the cottage flooding back. It seemed so long ago although it had only been a day or two before.

As Jodi sank into delicious warmth, Safronne stood beside her looking down, her legs set apart, her hips swinging slightly to push her pubis out. Then to Jodi's surprise she began to peel off her skin-tight garment, letting a pair of well-formed breasts ease out. Her navel was a long, deep oval in a cushion of soft, brown flesh which undulated with a quite hypnotic rhythm as the silk slipped past her hips.

Jodi's heart was pounding. Was this a striptease to titillate her senses even more? She watched the pulsing navel and lay still.

Another surprise met her eyes as the scarlet silk dropped lightly to the floor. Safronne's mons was bare, a totally hairless triangle of baby-smooth, brown skin. Her Mount of Venus swelled out roundly from the valleys of her groin. At the lower tip, a deep crevice dived between long and shapely legs. Having this wonderfully vibrant young woman standing naked at the bath side stirred sensations deep inside her, the like of which she had never felt in front of any man.

As Safronne smiled and turned away, Jodi felt a pang of disappointment. She had wanted to reach out and touch the sleek and elegant girl.

Safronne stepped into a shower, her honey-brown skin soon glistening as the water flowed. The well-proportioned bottom shone in a warm cascade of droplets. Then Jodi took a breath as Safronne bent to wash her feet, the soft purse of her pussy swelling large between her legs. The smooth and fleshy lips seemed to pout as Jodi watched the water stream between them and away. She breathed deeply as she imagined putting her lips to them. For a moment she even pictured putting out her tongue to sense their texture, their suppleness and warmth. She looked away. This whole affair was becoming too distracting ... She slipped under the water of her bath, but she could not immerse completely, her breasts were so buoyant and full.

'Dry my back, please?' Safronne held the towel to her and turned. Jodi reached out and enclosed the slender back within pink folds. When Safronne bent and pushed her bottom out, Jodi slipped the towel between the legs and rubbed her gently, feeling the suppleness of her purse, smelling her female scent.

Jodi's heartbeat pounded. Her inner thighs began to tremble. Why did the woman's scent have that effect on her? She felt that curious excitement in her solar plexus that she'd had the first time a man had slipped his hand up the inside surface of her leg and fingered her through her cotton panties.

The spell was broken as Safronne turned. 'Thank you,' she said softly. Then she knelt close to Jodi and ran a long finger over her pubis with a thoughtful expression on her face. 'Would you like me to shave you?'

Jodi frowned.

Safronne smoothed it away with her finger. 'Do I displease you?'

Embarrassed, Jodi answered, 'I'm sorry, but I thought you said you were going to shave me.'

Safronne smiled again. 'Of course. Women in my country do not have such hair as yours. It's considered unfeminine.'

Jodi stood abruptly and stepped out of the bath, towering over the kneeling girl. 'But this is not your country.'

Safronne smiled again and ran her fingertips over Jodi's thighs. 'But if we are to be lovers, I would rather you were shaved.'

110

Jodi shook her head. 'Whatever gave you the idea that . . . ?'

'Will you not allow me to make love to you?' Safronne ran her hands over Jodi's flanks and put her warm mouth to her navel.

Jodi looked away. She had never imagined making love to any other woman, but this had seemed so natural.

She picked up the towel and went through to the bedroom, unable to say, Yes – I do want to make love with you. Her mind was in a whirl. Should she allow herself to become involved with this exotic creature? Her common sense said No. Her body cried out, Yes – just as it had said yes when Bentonne had pinned her to that tree. Yes, yes, yes! She needed some release for her awful tension.

She stood and dried herself, watching Safronne out of the corner of one eye. When the Asian beauty led her to the bed and laid her down, Jodi did not demure. She simply lay and let her room mate powder her all over.

The mirror above the bed showed her body fully. Her breasts were tight and flushed from the heat of the bath. The nimbuses seemed more than usually brown against the paleness of her powdered skin. The soft hands brought them to that hardness she had come to like so much. When Safronne spread her legs, Jodi opened them obediently, just as she had at bath time as a child. She watched the reflection of the dark pink gash of her vulva as Safronne spread it slightly before letting her fingers wander down the inside of her leg.

Jodi gave a little sigh of pleasure. Then she heard the shaver, and she felt its gentle vibration as Safronne stroked her mons. She watched the curls of golden hair as they tumbled between her legs, tickling her labia as they went.

Soon her mons was bare and smooth, but little golden whiskers still frizzed about her secret lips. As Safronne bent her leg back, she felt herself spread widely, and her labia vibrated nicely as the shaver did its work.

When the pink lips emerged from their beard of curls, they seemed larger and more succulent than they'd ever done before, and curiously cool.

Safronne knelt up on the bed, looking between Jodi's legs. She seemed eminently pleased with her handi-work and ran a forefinger slowly over Jodi's mons to ensure that it was smooth. When the finger drifted downward, and touched on Jodi's nub, it rose from its fleshy hood as if begging for the touch.

Safronne caressed again, with curiosity in her eyes; it was such a pleasant feeling. No man had ever contacted that part af her so reverently or so lightly. Their fingers had always probed to feel her depth, to gauge her wetness and to see how ready she was for them to fuck. Safronne's touch was there to give her pleasure, nothing more. It didn't demand to be touched in return.

Safronne took Jodi's hands and drew her to her feet. She stood her before the dressing mirror and draped the folds of an electric-blue garment over her shoulder. Her breasts swelled roundly. Their nipples were long and large and very stiff, and Jodi wanted to bend and take one in her mouth.

'Would you like to try the garment now, miss?' Safronne asked in a smooth, light tone as she held the silk up for Jodi to appraise. Again, it was as if nothing intimate had transpired between them. Then without waiting for a response, Safronne opened the zip of the one-piece suit and beckoned Jodi to step in.

The electric blue colour suited her fair complexion. It

was sheer, and so tight that it hugged every little detail of her form, the twin lobes of her pussy showing clearly at the crotch. Her nipples pushed out strongly through the silk. It looked as if her nudity had been sprayed with shimmering blue, leaving not one feature to the viewer's imagination.

'This is nice,' Safronne whispered. 'It makes you look very beautiful, miss. Will you wear it to the party tomorrow night?'

Jodi wasn't sure about that. It was a bit too revealing for her conservative taste. But she wasn't going to spoil the pleasure of the girl.

Safronne slid the garment down, making Jodi's breasts ease out with a little bounce as they were freed. The garment slipped over the inward curve of her flank and to her hips, hanging just above her mons. Stripping her naked to her crotch, the slender hands slid inside the silk and pushed it down. Jodi was mesmerised as her body was revealed, the dark, deep eyes of the Asian girl watching every inch.

When she stepped from the silky heap on the rug, Jodi felt more than naked now that she was shaven. When she caught Safronne eyeing the reflection of her face, Jodi wondered if the girl was trying to gauge her mood again, intent on detecting if she objected to being stripped and touched . . .

Her heart began to race as the slender hands slipped around her waist. She swallowed hard and pulled her belly in. She closed her eyes as Safronne's hands roved her abdomen and thighs. When they cupped the mound of her pubis, she didn't move, but spread her legs for the forefingers to probe her crevice, and as a finger touched her clitoris, she sighed.

Jodi squatted slightly as Safronne's beguiling fingers slipped between her legs, stroking the inside of her thigh while those of the other hand worked her clitoris from the front.

The thumb of the hand between her legs pushed gently through her labia. Jodi could feel how slippery she'd become and how sensitive it made her. She hardly felt the thumb move up inside her, but when it pressed her G spot, she moaned and moved her hips, yearning for strong contact. The Asian girl responded with a gentle pincer movement, her forefinger on Jodi's clit while the long thumb thrust inside her. She felt her tension rising, yet the probing was so gentle. There was no thrashing and no struggle. There were no grunted pleas of *Squeeze my cock wrth your lovely cunt*, or *Fuck me doll, I'm coming – ahh!* This was simple loving, refined and tastefully done. It was not being done in the darkness of her squalid little bedsit, but in the light of day as she watched herself responding in the full-length glass before her.

Jodi began to judder as the ffngers worked her strongly. My god, that was so nice. She began to swing her hips. Then little tremors of sheer delight rippled through her belly. Her thighs began to quiver as she bent her knees, opening herself to the masturbating fingers of the girl, watching her reflection as she thrust her pelvis out.

Jodi let out an expression of wonderful relief as her climax came. It was not a huge and juddering affair, but a pleasant, warming one. It was not the heaving, humping kind of orgasm that she had craved to have with Bentonne, but more than welcome just the same. Her body felt alive now. Her skin was warm and tingly. And she felt that she'd been loved, even though they had not kissed.

When the beguiling fingers slipped away, Jodi felt abandoned. But when they reached her breasts and held them lightly, anointing them with the essence of her coming, she felt so vibrant. As fingers and slender thumbs pulled her nipples gently, she leaned back and rested her head against her lover's cheek.

'You are very beautiful,' the soft voice whispered in her ear. 'While you stay here, I am going to make love to you and pamper you and massage your cares away and make your body come to life. Would you like that, darling?'

Chapter Nine

'WHERE'S BENTONNE?' JODI shot the question at Safronne, partly to distract her mind from the Asian girl's suggestion that they should become lovers, and partly because she had a nagging worry about Bentonne's fate.

She eyed the Asian beauty, and the almond eyes studied her in return. 'Do you love him, miss?'

Jodi frowned and stood up tall. 'Of course I don't. I'm just concerned that he isn't being mistreated.'

Safronne smiled. 'But why would Max want to hurt him? Are they not cousins?'

Yes, Jodi thought to herself; they're not only cousins but deadly enemies as well. She threw her hair back briskly. 'Then take me to Bentonne and let me see for myself.'

For a moment Safronne seemed to ponder the matter. Then she smiled. 'All right. But we must be discreet. That man Polders is dangerous. He might tell Max and make him angry with us both.'

Jodi narrowed her eyes. 'Too bad. Now, are you going to take me to Bentonne or not?'

'I will take you to him later, but please don't tell Max.'

Safronne took Jodi by the hand, guided her through a small door at the end of the upper corridor and up a tightly winding stair. At the top was a dusty passage with rough wood doors leading off it. Each door had a rusty grille through which the pungent scent of spices wafted. It was stiflingly hot from the summer sun beating on the roof.

'I think your friend is being kept up here,' Safronne whispered, looking behind her anxiously. They peeked quickly through each grille, Jodi's tension rising all the time.

In one room there were bulging sacks and coils of rope upon the rough-planked floor. Jodi noticed a large loading door, barred on the inside, and a pulley and rail on the ceiling. Many of the ancient houses in Amsterdam had those, still used for raising furniture in modern times.

They came to the last door and paused. What would she do if Bentonne were not there? Did it really matter?

Safronne shot Jodi a frightened glance and looked to make sure that they had not been followed. Jodi wiped her forehead. Apart from the stifling heat she was sweating from the fear of being caught. She didn't want to lose her bonus now.

The sight of the familiar figure sitting on a rusty bed made Jodi's heart falter for a second. He was naked and perspiring profusely, his blanket lying on the mattress. She took a breath as Safronne slid the door bolt.

'Do not be long, my love,' Safronne whispered. 'I will wait here and warn you if I hear anyone upon the stair.'

Although the door swung noisily, Bentonne did not turn. Maybe he thought it was Polders coming with some food.

'Dean,' Jodi whispered hoarsely, 'are you all right?'

He rose and turned and stared. Then he glowered at her darkly. As he shuffled forward, she saw that he was hobbled at the ankles, and his wrists were tied behind him still. Clearly, Maximillian wasn't risking having him escape.

'You slut,' he growled as he glared at her. 'I knew you were part of Max's plot. If my hands were free I'd put them around your pretty neck and throttle you.'

'You can think that if you like, but you're wrong.' As her sympathy dissolved, Jodi pulled herself up to full height. Despite two days' growth of beard, tousled hair and total nakedness, he still held the air of superiority she had disliked from the outset. Had that not been one reason why she had taken the assignment – to take someone of his sort down a peg or two?

Her belly was tight, her hands trembling so violently that she had to clasp them hard in front of herself to still them.

He looked at her disparagingly. 'All right – if you're not colluding with my cousin, why are you dressed in silks while I'm naked in this garret?'

'Because I haven't done anything to deserve the kind of treatment you do.'

He snorted. 'No, but I can imagine what you have done to "deserve" being dressed like an Asian tart. I expect you've screwed my cousin already to get in his good books.'

Jodi stilled her temper and whispered, 'Your cousin has been the model of propriety, Mr Bentonne. He didn't leap on me like you did. He didn't finger me in my bath, or pin me to the mat.' She couldn't stop the sarcasm as she said the words.

Bentonne's face paled. His eyes became glazed for a moment as if he were recalling something hurtful. Then he looked behind her at the open door. Quickly, she backed towards it. She was not going to be accused of letting him escape. Then she realised that the hobble on his ankles was fastened to the bed. It would only allow him to circuit the room.

Bentonne closed on her, coming within an arm's length. 'You're lying again, Jodi. I don't believe Max hasn't touched you.'

'Don't lecture me about being a liar. You certainly had me convinced that you were as white as white.'

He sneered. 'And what's that supposed to mean?'

'You know very well, so don't play the innocent with me.'

As he glared into her eyes she was determined not to look away. 'If you believe any stories my cousin has been spinning to cover up his double-dealing, you're more of a fool than I thought.'

The crack of her hand across his face resounded around the room. His head snapped to one side just as hers had done when he had hit her at the cottage. At that moment she felt even with him. She felt glad that his cheek was turning red, and that his eyes were watering.

He stared at her and shook his head. 'Christ, Jodi. What has happened to us?'

She stood back, acutely aware of his nudity, his penis hanging limp, his testes swinging as his belly pumped.

'Happened to us?' she croaked. 'There is no "us".'

He tried to come closer but his hobble would not let him. 'But at the cottage I thought that we had the beginnings of something very special.'

'Then you were wrong!' She shook her head violently, trying to stop tears flooding from her eyes.

He strained at the hobble and dragged the bed. This time she had her back to the wall and could not evade

119

him easily. But did she want to? His anger excited her. His nakedness while he was tied and relatively helpless started those thrills running up from between her legs again.

Now he was close – too close. As he put his lips to her forehead, he whispered, 'Then if I was so wrong about what we had, why are you crying?'

'Because I'm confused, you fool. And it's all your fault.' She pushed him away, spreading her fingers on his hot chest. But contact with his flesh only reminded her further of the intimate times she'd had with him.

'My fault?' he croaked, pushing back against her hands. 'If you hadn't led my cousin's henchmen to the cottage I wouldn't have ended up in this place.'

'And if you hadn't been such a horny brute' – she slapped his penis hard – 'you wouldn't have fallen into your cousin's trap.' She was surprised to find that his penis had swelled: anger running between them always seemed to make them both horny.

He looked at her coldly for a moment. 'You're right. I was a fool to let you seduce me.'

'*Me* seduce *you*? I suppose I imagined the way you played with me against that tree.'

He smiled grimly, as if recalling those scenes. 'Well, it didn't take much you get you begging for it, did it? The way you knelt in front of the fire and sucked my cock so hungrily was hardly the behaviour of an innocent young maid.' His penis was half hard now.

She looked away, the fire of embarrassment burning her cheeks. She knew that she had been carried away by her own passion, but she could not help that now.

She looked up at him again. 'All right. I admit I got a bit carried away. But—'

'But nothing, Jodi. Stop making excuses for yourself and get me out of here.'

She side-stepped smartly to the doorway, nearly colliding with Safronne. 'No – I won't. I can't.' Tears ran down her cheeks.

'What do you mean, you can't?' Anger rose to his face. 'For Christ's sake, you silly bimbo, undo these ties and get me out of this place. The Board will meet in two days' time, and I've got to stop my cousin's game.'

Jodi stiffened. 'Calling me a bimbo does nothing to endear you to me, Bentonne.' She glanced at his penis, curving up between them strongly now. The man was a horny, arrogant pig, and he was turning her on again.

Pushing aside an impulse to hit him, she backed out of the room. 'You can go to hell, as far as I'm concerned. I'm not getting caught up any longer in this ridiculous feud you have with Max.'

'So, it's "Max"- now, is it?' He threw his head back angrily and put his hands on his hips, setting his legs apart just as he had by the tree. His penis reared up rigidly, the tip of it trembling as his belly pumped.

Jodi swallowed hard, turned and marched off down the passage, but it was only when she reached the stair that she realised that she was alone. She turned and looked for Safronne but the girl was nowhere to be seen; she wondered if Bentonne had somehow grabbed her. He might hold her hostage to secure his release.

As she ran back along the passage, Jodi's mind was filled with images of Bentonne's hands around Safronne's neck, her silk suit ripped, her full breasts lolling out as she struggled to get away. Then she heard Bentonne's angry voice.

'Get away from me, you slut.'

Jodi stared as she saw him backing away from Safronne, the Asian girl's palm stretched towards his balls.

'But I only want to touch them,' she croaned. 'They

121

are so beautiful. And look how your penis rears right up, waiting for my mouth. Please let me make it spurt.'

'I said get away, you harlot,' Bentonne was genuinely alarmed. 'I'm not here to amuse you.'

'But I do not want to amuse myself with you, sir,' she crooned as she eased herself towards him. 'I wish to give you pleasure. It is what I am trained for.'

Jodi could not move. Safronne seemed to be mesmerised as she looked at Bentonne's shaft. Then she recalled how forward the girl had been with her. They had hardly been introduced before Safronne had fingered her, intimately. But Safronne had not wanted anything for herself. She had seemed bent on giving pleasure.

Jodi stepped into the room as Safronne lunged at Bentonne, pushing him back on to the bed. His ankle ties had caught up so that he was unable to evade her further. He could not kick out or use his hands to ward her off. His penis still reared, his balls drawn up tightly.

He tried to wriggle away as Safronne gripped his cock, seemingly so intent on it that she didn't notice Jodi. If she did, perhaps she didn't care. She began to masturbate Bentonne very slowly.

'Get off me, you slut!' he hissed, wriggling in vain against his bonds. 'You won't get anything from me.'

Safronne put her lips to the head of his penis, and Jodi felt a pang of jealousy run through her. Did she feel something for the bastard after all?

'But I shall get something from you, sir,' Safronne whispered. 'I shall make you sow your seed. And when it spurts high in the air, I shall drink my fill.'

'You'll never make me come, you siren,' Bentonne growled.

Safronne simply smiled, opened her mouth and breathed hotly on his cock.

Bentonne took a long breath as the bowed lips sucked on his glans. He put back his head and shut his eyes as if resigned to the outcome.

Jodi grimaced. She had been right about him being a horny brute; he didn't take much seducing. She was sure now that Maximillian had known that, and had calculated correctly that all that was required to lure his cousin from his stronghold would be an attractive, sensual woman.

Bentonne tried to pull his cock from the Asian beauty's mouth, his bonds cutting into his ankles as he strained to get away. Then Jodi realised that he had seen her.

'I suppose you think this is very amusing,' he snarled.

Jodi drew back, feeling ashamed of herself. Then she thought, if he knew she was there, why should she not watch? He had known she had been among the trees at the cottage but had still performed for her.

Safronne seemed not to have noticed the exchange as she licked his scrotum. His glans was glowing with the colour of her lip gloss, which spread further down his shaft as she worked it with her lips, making it look angry and causing it to swell up more.

Jodi closed her eyes for a moment; the sight was turning her on so much.

'Lie back and relax, my love,' Safronne crooned as she took her mouth from the rose-tinged shaft and ran her tongue tip deep between his balls.

'I said leave me alone, you harlot. I'm not some toy you can amuse yourself with.'

Safronne looked up, hurt. 'I do not toy with you. I am very serious. Please let me show you just how nice a woman's tongue can be.' She lapped slowly at the web of his penis, making it jerk. Jodi's heart pounded as a

123

bead of semen rose from the eye and trickled down the groove.

Safronne seemed to delight in this. She rubbed the bead away with the tip of her finger then took it to her lips. While she sucked, she closed her eyes as if savouring some great delicacy; now Jodi knew that Safronne was not doing this solely for the pleasure of the man.

Safronne began to knead at Bentonne's thighs and slip her fingers up his belly. When she found a spot between his navel and his pubic bone, she pushed her nail in deeply.

He let out a gasp and his penis surged.

Safronne pressed again, harder, making a deep depression in his flesh. Then as she pushed, his penis rose, springing with its tension. She began to push and lick together; each push made it spring, each lick made it swell.

Jodi could not stop a tremor running up the insides of her legs and into her vagina. It was worse than being toyed with by the man and then abandoned. She wasn't even being included while another woman enjoyed her man.

Her man? He wasn't her man. He hadn't been 'her man' when he had cornered her in the forest and touched her up in the bath. He had already been the man of a dozen other women. Was that not how he had built such a reputation as a womaniser? There was no smoke without fire, and it appeared that Bentonne was easily set alight.

As he lay back and strained his cock for the girl to tongue, he began to pant.

Jodi found herself panting, too. Her belly tightened as his penis tensed. Then a fountain af semen shot right up his torso, and two more spurts in quick succession reached up to his shoulders.

Thrusting out her breasts, the Asian girl let out a long, low moan. Then her belly panted and her breasts began to shake.

'Hell,' Jodi whispered to herself, 'she's come as well.'

Now Safronne licked him like a cat would lick a plate of milk. She lapped him from his testes and up his beating shaft, working the tip of her snaking tongue around his rosy glans. Then she licked him from his pubis to his navel. Long strokes of her tongue rasped his heaving belly, wetting the same fine hairs that Jodi's fingers had delighted so much in stroking.

Safronne's lapping seemed to make him tremble more. 'Bitch,' he whispered hoarsely, 'you crazy bitch.'

'But did I please you, sir?' she asked looking briefly into his eyes before she licked his nipples one by one.

'No – you damned well didn't please me,' he fumed, lying back to let her lick his neck. 'If you really want to please me, untie my legs and arms.'

'Free you? So that you might hold me down and fuck me with this thing?' She laughed, ringing his still-hard shaft to squeeze thick drops of semen from its eye before she covered it with her mouth.

'Free me so I can get out of this place and stop my cousin's crazy bid for power.'

Safronne sat back and admonished him with one look. 'But then your cousin would be angry with me.'

'I'd reward you well,' he said softly.

'And how would you reward me, master?' she asked with great amusement. 'Would you push this deep into my bottom and make me wriggle on it while you pulled my tits?'

'I'd give you more money than my cousin does,' he croaked as she sucked a testicle.

Safronne laughed. 'But how do you know if he pays me any money at all? Perhaps I live here just so he can use me whenever he likes. Maybe I lie in my bed at night, desperate for him to come and tie me up. Can you not imagine how he gags me and spanks my bottom to make me wriggle while he fucks me from behind? Can you not picture him making me kneel to take the whole of his long, hard cock into my mouth, while he fills me with the seed that I adore?' She dipped a finger into Bentonne's navel then took it to her lips.

'Then you're nothing but a whore.'

'I would be if that were true,' she laughed. As she stroked Bentonne's wet scrotum, it was clear to Jodi that the girl was playing with him wickedly.

He sat up angrily. 'Stop that, you minx. You've made me come. Now untie me or I swear that when I do get loose, I'll . . .'

His eyes lit up with hope as Safranne knelt to touch the ties tangled around the bed frame. But his expression turned to anger when she rose. She set her head back and laughed aloud. 'I'm sorry, sir. I was simply checking that your bonds are tight. Now, if you will excuse me, I must take Miss Barens down to dinner with *Mijnheer*.'

Jodi stepped back smartly, feeling herself blush as Safronne swept out past her. But she stopped and put her lips to Jodi's and whispered through the kiss, 'Did you like that, darling, or did it make you angry?'

Jodi studied the oval face for some seconds. 'Did you do it to make me jealous?'

Safronne frowned. 'But why would you be jealous if you do not care for him?'

Jodi lowered her eyes, knowing that she'd been caught out.

Safronne bolted the door and took Jodi's arm, ushering her towards the stairs. 'No, I did not wish to make you jealous. I become uncontrollably aroused when I see a man's cock pumped up like a banana. I cannot stop myself from taking it in my mouth. But only when he spurts his seed does my body orgasm. Did you not see that?'

Jodi nodded, feeling sheepish at such candour.

'And did it not make you feel excited?'

Jodi looked into her eyes. 'It made me more excited than I would have imagined.' Pleased at her newfound candour, she continued. 'I nearly came as well.'

Safronne smiled broadly, pleased that Jodi had enjoyed the scene. She put her mouth close to Jodi's ear and whispered, looking up and down the corridor first. 'And did you want to burst in and stretch yourself over his cock?'

Jodi took a long, deep breath. Then she simply nodded.

'Good. I'm pleased that you were so aroused, my love. And if you enjoy watching and doing such things, I think you will like the party we are going to have tomorrow.'

Jodi felt her eyes go wide. 'Is it going to be that kind of party?'

'A good party is one that pleases everyone. If the guests want talk about politics, they are most welcome. But if the men want to chase and roll and fuck anyone they like, they may. Should the girls want to suck off all the men, they are free to do so, too.'

Jodi could feel colour rising to her cheeks again. She had never taken part in any orgy.

Safronne smiled and brushed Jodi's cheek. 'And you, my lover, will be very welcome to join in anything you like.'

Jodi did not respond. Perhaps she would simply watch the others having fun.

At eight o'clock Safronne guided Jodi down to dinner.

The dining room reflected the opulent tastes of the owner. Large and spacious, it was dominated by a huge table set with shining silver and lit by chandeliers. The polished floor was spread with oriental carpets and around the panelled walls hung paintings of old Dutch scenes. Had it not been for the long-cased clock standing in one corner, proclaiming the hour of eight, Jodi would have lost all sense of time.

She turned to see Safronne studying her carefully. Was the girl anxious that her appearance should please Van de Rohe? She smiled and made the little bow Jodi had become accustomed to. '*Mijnheer* – I mean *Mr* Van de Rohe – will be with you shortly.'

For an instant, Jodi felt relieved. The girl had presumed that she did not understand Dutch. She felt quite alone as Safronne left. She turned to a small, round table in one corner to see that it had places set for two. So – Maximillian intended that they should dine alone. Now she was on edge. At any moment that door would open and he would enter. What would he say? Would the time spent with her alone be a subtle interrogation to see just how much she knew about Bentonne and his dealings? Or would a candle-lit dinner for two be his first step towards getting her into his bed?

When the door did open and close, Jodi did not look up immediately. Instead, she toyed with a silver knife, watching her reflection. Then with all the poise that she could muster, she raised her eyes towards the door.

Maximillian Van de Rohe looked magnificent. Dressed in an immaculate white tuxedo, which showed the depth of his smooth tan well, he looked far more handsome than Bentonne had looked at his best.

'Good evening, Jodi,' he said softly as he took her

hand and kissed it. 'You look incredibly beautiful – and very sexy, if I may say so.'

'You may, but it won't get you anywhere,' she said sharply, but regretted it immediately.

He frowned slightly, then seemed to brush the remark aside, pulling back a chair for her to sit on.

She sat, feeling quite genteel in the opulence of the setting. This was so different to the scene she had shared with Bentonne when they had sat naked, supping stew .

'And how was your afternoon, Jodi?' Max lit the candles with a gold lighter and sat back to contemplate her. It was not a harsh appraisal, more one of admiration. Working a remote control, he dimmed the chandeliers so that he and Jodi were isolated from the room in a pool of flickering candle-light.

'I slept most of the afternoon,' she said coolly. 'Then I read for a while.' She was a bit on edge now. Did he have any idea of what she had really been up to? Was her face flushed from watching Safronne with Bentonne? Or was the simple fact that she needed a cock between her legs the reason why she was so nervous of Van de Rohe, as she looked at him demurely?

The quietness between them was broken as Safronne entered with a trolley laden with food. She served them both with delicious-looking dishes nestled in beds of spicy rice, and then withdrew with her usual bow.

Questions welled in Jodi's mind as they began to eat. She held them down for a while before she blurted, 'What made you and Bentonne become such enemies?'

Max looked at her for a while. 'Dean always was a dark one. He always cheated in any game we played. He hated losing – especially to me. We used to vie over childish things, but later it became more serious. When we were in our early twenties he used to get furious when I got the girls and he got left out.'

'You fought for the same girls?' Jodi sipped her wine, pleased that she was getting the man to open up.

He smiled and his eyes twinkled. 'Can I help it if they found me more attractive, and more satisfactory as a lover?' He looked at her intently.

She noted the way he emphasised the word 'satisfactory', and wondered how satisfactory he might be compared with the man tied up in his attic. Bentonne had certainly been unsatisfactory as far as Jodi was concerned. Even now, she was angry from her unfulfilling encounters with him.

She took a long breath and tried to quell the feelings developing inside her. She could feel her nipples poking through the silk of her suit and was sure that the Dutchman would have noticed.

Jodi sipped her wine again. 'Isn't it a bit petty to let your personal differences interfere with business?'

He looked up and smiled. 'Not when the man has been cheating the company and blaming the losses on me. He seems to have a need to destroy me at any cost.'

'But that doesn't give you the right to keep him locked up, does it?' She was aware of the crack in her voice, but didn't care.

'Let's just say that he is under house arrest until I present the findings of my investigations to the Board.' He touched her hand across the table. 'Don't worry about it, Jodi. I shall put you both on the first available flight back to England just as soon as the Board have made their deliberations. You do believe me, don't you?'

She nodded.

'Good. Now – eat Safronne's delicious food. She will be most offended if we let it go cold. Don't you think she's a wonderful cook?'

His hand on hers felt warm and reassuring and she began to relax again. 'OK. Sorry if I've been a pain over this.'

'You don't need to apologise, sweetheart,' he said softly, pouring her more wine.

She warmed to him calling her 'sweetheart', just as she had warmed to Safronne calling her 'darling'.

The meal went quickly after that, Van de Rohe keeping the conversation very general. His easy manner, the good food and fine wines completely submerged any misgivings she still had about his treatment of Bentonne. The man would get his comeuppance and that would be that. She resolved to enjoy the next few days. Then life would return to normal and, in a few weeks, it would be difficult to believe that the whole affair had ever taken place.

'What do you do with yourself in the evenings, Jodi?' He asked it as they sat on a cavernous sofa drinking coffee laced with brandy.

Her train of thought was broken, for the blue eyes looking over his cup seemed hypnotic, wooing her with their softness. The way his mouth curved knowingly at the corners made her thrill. Was he really asking what she liked to do in bed? Was he going to lean over to kiss her, or move in on her and slip his hand between her legs?

She swallowed hard. 'What do I do?'

'After you get home from a hard day's work and change into something comfortable?' He poured her more coffee, still smiling slightly.

'That depends if I'm alone or not,' she said, unwilling to tell him what he clearly wanted to know. Being candid with Safronne was quite different to being candid with this man, no matter how attractive she found him.

'If I am alone, I play tennis in the summer, or go to the health club.'

He put his head back in acknowledgement, playing her game. 'What do you do at the health club?'

'I swim. Work out. Use the hot tub. Sometimes I go in the sauna.'

'And would you like to work out now or take a swim? Or use my hot tub and sauna perhaps? They are already on. I always go down to unwind after a hard day.'

Jodi knew that he'd cornered her. He'd called her bluff and won. She couldn't very easily back out now. But then she didn't want to.

'OK.' She smiled. 'I'm game.'

Maximillian Van de Rohe was magnificent. Stripped naked, he stood beneath the shower before getting into the hot tub.

Jodi's pulses raced.

He hadn't turned a hair as he'd removed his dinner clothes. From her position at the edge of a small but luxurious swimming pool, Jodi watched him out of the corner of her eye while she sipped a coke. The brandy in the coffee had made her deliciously mellow and totally uninhibited.

When he bent to wash his toes, she had a clear view of his testes through his legs. They hung loosely, frizzed about with very fair hair. He was a true blond.

'Coming in?' he called, striding to the tub. He stood at the edge, putting in one foot, his penis wagging to the movement. Even though flaccid, it was very long, and Jodi wondered what it might be like when angry . . . Then she smiled to herself, certain that she would soon find out. He stood beside her, self-assured and

132

unabashed, and she realised why Maximillian Van de Rohe was so successful with women.

'Coming in?' he called again as he sank down in the tub. 'If you're shy, you can keep your knickers on.' He grinned widely.

Jodi pretended to be offended. She turned for him to undo the zip of her blue silk suit. Then she turned again and slipped out of it. She wore no bra or panties and her breasts eased out as she pulled it off her shoulders. Then she paused, letting him view her navel. When she let the sheer material float to the floor, his eyes opened widely. It was only then that she remembered that Safronne had shaved her mount.

He looked at her knowingly as she glanced down and saw that his penis was larger as he slipped into the tub. From his position below her, Jodi knew that the crevice of her pussy would be clear for him to see.

She was beginning to suspect why Safronne had shaved her. Her master clearly liked a woman smooth and hairless. But in Jodi's mellow mood, it didn't really matter. In any case, she was proud of the form between her legs, and widened them to let him see it better.

Chapter Ten

THE WATER OF the hot tub bubbled and tickled between Jodi's legs, adding to the sensations already gathering there. After a cool swim, the water felt even hotter.

She sat opposite Van de Rohe, her legs entwined with his, soft music in the background and low lights making the whole scene utterly romantic.

'Did you enjoy your swim?' he asked, looking at her steadily.

She nodded. 'It was nice. It's a really lovely pool.'

It was small talk and they both knew it. He was not making innuendoes about her nudity or her willingness to mate. Neither was he making any reference to the fact that his penis was fully erect, the tip of it poking pinkly above the water. When she looked across at him it came into her field of view.

She closed her eyes and took a long, deep breath as she sank into the heat.

'Are you glad you stayed, Jodi?'

She smiled her acknowledgement.

'Good. I'm very pleased you did. It isn't often I have the pleasure of such intelligent and attractive female company.'

She looked at him askance. 'I find that difficult to believe.'

He shrugged. 'But it is true. Would you like to sauna now?'

She couldn't say no. She guessed that this whole thing had been a challenge from the start to see just how far she would go. Well, she'd show him that she wasn't prudish, but she was still not totally certain if she would make love with him or not. As time went on it was becoming much more likely even though he hadn't made a move. He had simply ignored his erection as if it were quite normal for a man to have a huge horn sticking out like that.

When he stood up, he towered over her, and she could not help looking up at his balls with the water running off them. It reminded her poignantly of Bentonne in the rain. She took his hand as he reached down for her own. Then he led her to the sauna box, his head held up as proudly as his cock.

The sauna box was very hot. Sitting opposite him on the lower bench, she could not ignore the shaft which lay against his belly, the tip of it almost at his navel. But still he did not look at it.

'Tell me about your work,' he said, ladling water on the stones. The scented steam made her burn delightfully all over. Her sweat ran down her neck, trickling between her breasts.

'I used to do safaris in Africa,' she said casually as she brushed her hair back, making her breasts swing freely. 'I enjoyed tracking game for visitors to see.'

'And why don't you do that now?' He moved his position, making his penis wag. His balls spread out across the bench, bulging in their sac.

'I had to come back to England when my mother was ill. I've been tracking unfaithful lovers for the agency

135

since that time. But I think you already know that. Didn't you get a thorough dossier on me from the agency?'

He smiled. 'They told me everything I needed know about you for the job I had in mind.'

But had they told him she spoke his language, she wondered?

'Would you like to return to tracking wildlife, Jodi?' He touched his penis but only, it appeared, to run the perspiration from its length.

'Of course,' she said, somewhat distracted by it. 'But I would need a lot of capital to start up on my own.'

'Would you let me finance you?'

'What would you want to do that for?'

He shrugged. 'Perhaps I still feel a little guilty about the way you were treated before we met.'

She studied him hard. The perspiration beading on his pectorals and running down his belly to his pubis only served to distract her more, and to focus her attention right back on his cock.

'So what do you say to my proposal, Jodi?'

She looked him in the eyes. 'What would you expect to get from me in return?'

'A free safari, perhaps?'

Now she looked at him warily. 'Nothing else?'

'Like expecting you to be my mistress, do you mean?'

She let her expression of doubt answer that one.

He leaned across to her. 'Nothing could be further from my thoughts. Surely you don't think I want to screw you, do you?'

Hell, she thought, if he didn't want to screw her, why was he sitting here with such an enormous hard-on?

She stared him out. 'Don't you?'

'Don't I what?'

'Don't you want to fuck me?' The brandy had made

her bold and flattened any inhibitions she might have had.

'Would you like me to?' His eyes twinkled as he watched her, and she was sure his phallus twitched.

Damn him, he was toying with her. By playing cool, he was making her want him more – and he knew it.

'I asked the question first,' she said, determined not to be the first to answer.

'I can screw anyone I like, Jodi, whenever I like.'

'I'm sure you can. But that's evading the question,' she said rather sharply.

'Of course,' he smiled. 'But surely you don't expect me to tell you in words what I want from you tonight?'

'Why not?'

'Because I am more refined than to tell a lady exactly what I want to do with her.'

'But if I weren't a lady?' she smirked, her eyes alight with the fun he was creating.

'Then I might say, lie down and show me your cunt. I want to lick around it and make it really wet before I fuck it hard. But since you are a lady, I wouldn't dream of saying such a thing.'

Her heart beat strongly as he grinned. She was enjoying his game. He was so boyish, so good-looking, so cool in his manner – and he was so horny. She was beginning to want to behave like Safronne had with Bentonne. But dare she make the first move? She began to wonder just how long it would be before she had to.

Now it was she who grinned. 'But now you've started to confess your deepest desires, why don't you continue?'

He reflected her grin. 'What – and tell you that I want to have you suck my penis while I thrash your back and bottom with this switch?' He picked up a bunch of whippy twigs and thwacked them across his palm.

Jodi blanched. She had never been birched before. 'Go on,' she whispered, needing him to say more about his fantasies. The man was revealing what he really felt, instead of playing clandestine games to arouse her interest.

He switched playfully at her legs.

'Don't you dare,' she giggled and put her legs up on the bench. But this only served to expose her labia to him; they were squashed together tightly.

He switched her again.

She got up and tried to fend him off, but he turned her so that her knees were on the floor and her breasts were on the bench.

Now he began to whip her bottom lightly, and stroke the twigs right up between her legs.

For a moment she knelt obediently, feeling like some wanton slut who deserved a thorough whipping. However, not wishing to appear to be too subservient, she turned away and rose, but he pushed her down on to her back. The bench was hot against her skin, and it served only to increase her inner heat.

Now he towered over her, his leg between her own, his knee perilously close to her crotch. She wanted to feel his sweating flesh slip between her labia. They were so slick from the heat and her arousal.

He stroked her belly and her breasts and made her wriggle. The feeling was delightful as the twigs whisked across her nipples, making them stand proud. She made a pretence of escaping, but he pushed her down. She wriggled more to no avail, his fingers slipping from her shoulders to her breasts, both slick with sweat.

He hung there for a moment, her breasts cupped in his palms, the nipples poking out between his fingers. She wound her legs around his hips and tried to pull him down.

138

Now it was he who feigned resistance, his penis wagging as he tried to get away.

'No, don't, Jodi!' He laughed.

'Why not?' She giggled. 'You know you want to.'

'Want to what?'

'You want to shaft me with that.'

'Do I?'

'Yes, you do.' As she pulled him with her legs, he lost his grip and landed on her.

Now she wound her legs tightly round his hips. His mouth came down on hers. 'And how do you like to be fucked, Miss Barens?' he whispered through the kiss.

'Any way you like,' she groaned as she felt his penis press against her vulva. Then it was in her, so slippery and so strong. She felt its hardness as it rippled up inside her, nudging past her G spot and fathoming her depth. It was so, so nice.

He began to flex his hips and work her strongly. 'Do you like to be fucked like this?'

She whispered, 'Yes!'

'Not harder, like this?' He drove in almost brutally and took her breath away.

'Yes,' she gasped, 'like that as well.'

He laughed, driving his cock in hard.

She giggled when the wet hair of his scrotum tickled against the membranes of her loins as she spread her legs and stretched herself for him.

'Oh, god!' she gasped. 'That's nice. You don't know how nice!'

Thrusting in and holding, his pubis squashed against her nub. 'But is it as nice as when my cousin fucked you in front of that fire?' he gasped as he drove again.

'Much, much nicer,' she rasped.

'And is this bigger than Dean's?' he asked, raising himself on his hands and looking down between her legs as he pulled his penis out, then thrust it in strongly.

It was a while before she answered, as she squeezed him hard, trying to sense him all. 'Much bigger,' she sighed at last. 'I think I can feel it right up to my navel.'

He kissed her again and pushed her legs back hard. She looked down through the mounds of her breasts and across the slick plain of her belly to see his shaft withdraw. Then he began to saw it through the valley of her pussy, the helmet pushing hard against her nub. She watched with awe as the head appeared above her shaven mons, swollen with his tension, straining as he thrust. He bowed his back and closed his eyes, and she watched his cock stiffen, then spurt a jet of fluid up between her breasts. The second spurt landed on her neck, and the third one reached her mouth.

Instinctively, she licked her lips, the salty taste of semen blending with her sweat.

He rested then, between her legs, the contractions of his climax transmitting to her vulva. She wriggled to feel it better and bring herself to climax.

Now he spread his semen an her belly and began to work it into her breasts and then her neck, making her even slicker than she was. He knelt and pushed her legs back, looking down between them. With long and elegant fingers, he squeezed his cock and took its issue to her swollen cleft, massaging at the hollows of her loins. He wiped the tip deeply through her labia, painting them and spreading them, making her want more.

Jodi's climax came in spasms, accompanied by a rush of heat and the flush of her own fluids. It was a great relief, although she would have preferred to have his cock inside her, to feel it spurt and beat.

He sat astride her torso and rubbed his balls between her breasts, slipping in her perspiration and the slickness of his semen. He worked her nipples with his thumbs and had her lick his penis from his testes to the glans. She took it in her mouth, and made him come again, pumping strongly against her tongue. Then she sat up on the bench and sucked him as he stood, kneading her hair with his fingers, and whispering, '*Mmm* that's nice!'

He took her around the back and legs and ran into the pool. They laughed and splashed as they ducked each other, washing their bodies clean. Jodi took refuge in a floating pneumatic chair but he quickly tipped her off. Once or twice his cockshaft slipped inside her, and she wriggled on it briefly before he pulled it out.

He dried her long and carefully, kissing her all over, from the backs of her knees to her anus, up to her breasts and finally reaching her lips. He sat between her legs as she bent and touched her toes, gobbling at the soft flesh of her pussy. Darting his tongue between its lips, he almost made her come, before he migrated to her anus and licked it very slowly. He bit her inner thighs and the membranes of her groin, then smacked her bottom hard, telling her how wanton she had been.

Then he lifted her and took her through a changing room, a small but well-appointed gym, up several flights of stairs and to his bed.

They lay close and warm together, his arms around her shoulders, his thigh between her legs, pressing hard into the soft flesh of her pussy. Then he kissed her lightly as he whispered, 'My god, Miss Barens, you are beautiful. I think I may be in danger of falling in love with you.'

Chapter Eleven

THE DAY WAS bright when Jodi woke and stretched, alone in Max's bed.

She skipped into the bathroom and took a long, hot shower. As the water trickled down her breasts and off her nipples, they swelled. When it ran between her legs, seeking out her crevice, she set her feet apart and put her head back in the flow. It felt so good to have the heat down there. She was feeling quite aroused already. Although she'd climaxed in the sauna, he had worked her up again and not released her tension.

Jodi went naked back to Safronne's room, not caring if she was seen. She dressed in a pair of designer jeans and a pale pink sweater, which Safronne had lent her. Then she stood before the mirror and pushed her breasts out hard until she could see the nipples clearly. As she pulled the jeans up tight, the bulges of her secret lips showed plainly at her crotch.

She smiled, recalling how she had watched Max's eyes as she had bared herself by the hot tub. He had said that she was the best company he had had for a long time. Unlike that bastard Bentonne, he thought she was intelligent as well as very sexy.

I think I'm in danger of falling in love with you.

The words ran through her head as she made her way down to breakfast. Those were the most romantic words she could recall any man saying to her. Had Bentonne been as chivalrous, as much fun and as romantic, she might have been more concerned about him. But now that she had got to know Max better, she was sure that he would never hurt a soul.

She found the stairs that led to the sauna and pool, but turned instead towards the kitchens, where Safronne was busy at the stove.

They kissed; and as they kissed, Safronne slipped her fingers over Jodi's breast and rubbed the nipple. It was not a lascivious touch but an intimate greeting from a friend.

'And did you sleep well, my love?' Safronne asked as she stroked a hair from Jodi's face.

'Very well, thanks.'

'I am glad.' Safronne put her arms around Jodi's shoulders and held her tightly.

Jodi smiled and kissed her neck, whispering, 'You make me feel so safe.'

Safronne smiled. 'I am pleased. I want you to feel safe here. I want you to feel free enough to express yourself in any way you please.'

Jodi guessed that meant that Safronne wanted her to be uninhibited in bed. When Safronne ran a finger between Jodi's legs, skimming the denim that covered up her pussy, Jodi knew her deduction was correct.

Safronne kissed her nose. 'Would you like some breakfast?'

Jodi sat at a long pine table laden with a huge variety of cheeses, cooked meats and delicious-looking breads.

'Did you fuck?' Safronne called out casually as she boiled a couple of eggs.

Jodi turned to see the dark eyes watching her from the stove.

She nodded.

'Did he fuck you hard enough?' Safronne asked, as she set the eggs on Jodi's plate.

Jodi nodded again, aware of the heat creeping up her neck.

'But you didn't come.'

'What makes you say that?'

'I can see it in your eyes, my love.'

Jodi's blush reached her cheeks. 'I didn't come as well as I needed to.'

Safronne stroked her cheek. 'I know what that is like. Many times I do not come even when he fucks me very hard.'

'But why don't you make him be more considerate?' Jodi asked, surprised at the anger in her voice.

'Because he is my master, and he is a man.'

'To hell with being a man. Why shouldn't they wait for us?'

'But it is their nature,' Safronne whispered, stroking Jodi's breast. 'We cannot change them.'

'But we can tie them up and have them the way we want them.' She smiled to think how exciting it had been having Bentonne tied to the bunk in that cellar.

The day went very quickly. They both worked in the kitchens on the buffet for the party and later arranged the table in the dining room. While Safronne polished silver, Jodi did the flowers, humming happily to herself all the time.

At seven o'clock they started to prepare themselves for the party. Stepping from the shower, Safronne looked more radiant than ever. Jodi wrapped her in a towel and patted her dry. From behind the Asian girl, she slipped her hands under her arms and cupped her breasts, eager to let Safronne know just how attracted to her she was.

Safronne's breasts felt wonderfully mobile in Jodi's outstretched palms. The nipples burgeoned strongly between her fingers as she plucked them, and Safronne gave out little sounds of pleasure. Jodi slipped the towel around the shapely legs and rubbed their brown skin dry. Safronne spread her feet as Jodi put her hand between her legs, sawing the soft towel gently between them and pulling it up Safronne's back and over her curving belly.

When Safronne bent to dry her toes, Jodi found her face level with her bottom. Those lush, full labia pouted out at her again, inviting her to kiss them.

Jodi breathed in deeply as she put her lips to them.

Safronne turned and pushed her mount at Jodi's face then drew her to the bed. She lay on her back and opened her legs to show herself off fully.

As Jodi knelt to study the female form before her, her own moist lips began to throb. Also naked from her shower, Jodi spread her knees and felt a draught between her legs, cooling the heat that grew there.

Now she ran her forefingers up her roommate's thighs, pushing the long legs back to gain access to the hollows of her loins. Her fingers trembled as they reached the large purse of Safronne's sex and stretched the skin until it blanched. Moisture welled from Safronne as Jodi spread her widely and ran her lips down one side of the fleshy mouth. She kissed one plump lip with tenderness then traversed up the other, sucking Safronne's clitoris as she passed.

Safronne moaned and wriggled under the sensuous touch and pulled her legs back to stretch her anal ring. Gently she ran a fingertip around it; Safronne juddered to each touch. As Jodi stroked, the Asian girl reached down a long, slim finger to work her clitoris slowly in small circles, while the fingers of the other hand plucked a stiffened nipple.

When Jodi kissed her pubis, Safronne pressed her belly, whispering, 'Lick my cunt, my sweetest, fuck me with your tongue.'

'There's no time for that,' Jodi said quite sternly, as she stroked a small mole between Safronne's vulva and her loin. 'We've got to go down for the party soon.'

Safronne looked down at her and pouted. 'But it is so nice. Just lick me once.'

With her hands shaking and her belly tight, Jodi put her head between the outstretched legs. The purse of flesh was yawning so wide that she could see its inner lips. She put her mouth to them and felt her roommate tense.

Safronne came with violent little shudders, the lips of her pussy opening and closing slowly. As the orgasm grew in strength, Jodi closed her eyes and pressed her mouth against the lips, while Safronne wound her legs around Jodi's neck, trapping her in a sea of pulsing flesh.

Jodi flushed. Her belly tensed and a series of rippling tremors went right through her. She pressed her breasts against the bed, rubbing the nipples as roughly as she could. Then curling a finger inside herself, she worked her nubbin slowly until her pulses ceased.

When Safronne's orgasm had passed as well, she released Jodi from her hold. She raised herself and grinned. 'I think we ought to dress, don't you?'

Safronne dressed in red and Jodi in her body-hugging blue. Safronne slid the full-length zip right up to Jodi's breasts, which bulged nicely through the silk, and her pubis showed quite clearly once again.

They fixed their makeup and looked each other up and down with wide, admiring eyes.

'I think the guests will like you very much,' Safronne whispered through a fleeting kiss. Then she took Jodi by the hand and led her down the stairs.

Jodi's heart beat strongly. She was not quite sure what Safronne meant by the guests liking her 'very much' . . .

Chapter Twelve

THE GUESTS ARRIVED in ones and twos. None was over forty and they all looked very prosperous. The men wore smart tuxedos, and the elegant women were dressed in low-cut gowns or in slinky cat-suits. One tall, dark-haired woman wore a purple caftan flecked with gold. As she wafted through the doorway, it came undone to show that she was naked underneath.

The men viewed Jodi discerningly, while the women raised their noses.

Max Van de Rohe took Jodi's hand and led her around the dining room where the buffet had been laid. He introduced her to everyone in English. Coming to the last few guests, Jodi looked up to find the mischievous eyes of her young captor locked on to hers.

'This is Hans,' Max said. 'But I forgot – you two have met.'

Jodi trembled as Hans put her hand to his lips and kissed it tenderly. Closely shaved and dressed in a white tuxedo, he was suave and far too handsome for her liking. Such good-looking men turned her to jelly as they raked her up and down with searching eyes. She recalled only too well having him look at her in that cellar as she beguiled him with her nakedness. She shook herself from the memories and fixed Hans's eyes as he straightened from his bow.

'Hello, Jodi,' he said in a soft, almost romantic way. 'How have you been since you almost killed me?'

Jodi raised an eyebrow and looked at Max, but his attention was diverted. Safronne came up with a tray of pink champagne.

Hans put his arm around the girl and kissed her on the forehead. 'Hello, Safronne, you delicious creature. You look as sexy as ever tonight. What strenuous games have you in store for us?'

Safronne smiled the demurest little smile and fluttered her long lashes. 'That is a surprise, Master Hans. You must eat the first course and build up your strength. Only then might you be allowed to sample the sweets.' She did her little bow and moved on gracefully just as the tall woman in the flowing purple caftan moved in on the group.

'Are you not going to introduce me, Maxi?' she boomed in cultured Dutch.

Max took Jodi's hand; the woman looked her up and down. 'This is Jodi Barens,' he said in English. 'But she does not understand our language. Jodi, this is Maria Hagen.'

Jodi tried to smile while the woman scanned her body, the black eyes stopping at her pubis for rather longer than they ought to have.

'And what do you like, Jodi, my dear?' she whispered behind her hand.

The words grated on Jodi. The woman was only a few years older than herself but she held such an air of superiority in her manner and her looks.

'What do I like?' she queried, not quite certain what the woman was angling for.

The woman took her out of earshot and whispered,

149

'Perhaps I should have asked, whom do you like?'

Jodi looked her straight in the eyes. 'I don't know what you mean.'

Maria Hagen smiled. 'I think you do. You are clearly here to amuse us. What tricks do you perform?'

Jodi pulled her arm away. 'I don't "perform" any "tricks". Now, if you'll excuse me, I'll see if Safronne needs my help.'

Maria caught her arm. 'Bravo, my sweet. I like a girl who spins out the mystery. I'd like to get to know you better.'

Jodi held her gaze and tried to calm herself. 'I don't think that will be possible. I'm leaving in a day or two.'

Maria set her head back and laughed. 'Perhaps you are, but rest assured we will know you better before the party's finished. We will know every crevice and mound of your lovely body, Miss Barens. Several women here have got their eyes on you already. Have you not noticed how the Countess Dehousen has been looking at you for the past ten minutes?' She nodded towards a stunning woman of about thirty, dressed in an azure gown of shimmering silk, her blond hair sparkling with a small tiara. As Jodi caught her eyes, she smiled demurely, then sipped at her champagne.

Jodi's hands were shaking as she helped herself to food. She didn't look up when someone came to her side.

'You look pale. Are you all right?' Hans touched her arm as they both reached for the same vol-au-vent. When she withdrew quickly, he put it on her plate.

'Thanks,' she mumbled, annoyed at herself for blushing. 'I'm OK. Why did you ask?'

'You looked nervous. Has Kruella been needling you?'

'Kruella?'

He smiled. 'Maria Hagen, my dear.' They both laughed at his imitation of the woman. His eyes shone as he looked into hers. 'Don't worry. Her bark's worse than her bite. She's really quite insecure underneath her haughty manner.'

'And who's the woman in the tiara?'

Hans looked casually around, then smirked. 'That is Anna, the Countess Dehousen. Why? Do you fancy her?'

Jodi gave him a nudge.

'From the way she's been looking at you, I think she fancies you, Jodi. Look how she's smiling at you now.'

Jodi turned away. The beautiful woman was studying her and she felt unaccountably excited.

'Some say she's a masochist,' Hans whispered. 'I believe she likes being tied up and spanked.' He laughed softly, his eyes shining brightly as he looked closely at Jodi.

She stayed with Hans for an hour, chatting about his photographic skills and his university course. His having studied her minutely through the window of the cottage and in that cellar prison aroused her. Now that they were on different terms, Jodi liked him very much. She was sorry when he broke off their conversation and left the party to drive back to his university.

Jodi helped Safronne for a while until Max got up and banged the table. 'May I have your attention, ladies and gentlemen! The hubbub hushed. 'Now – if you've had your fill, it is time for the ladies to withdraw and the men to take their cigars and brandy to the recreation area.' All eyes turned on Jodi; she started to get worried. But Max took her arm and said softly, 'The men will go to the pool. Will you take the brandy and cigars down please? I've got some business to attend to. I'll see you later, my sweet.'

His touch on her arm and the expression in his eyes were reassuring. She was pleased he'd given her a useful task instead of expecting her to go into the drawing room with those haughty women.

Jodi took a tray with decanters and cigars to the basement, the men drifting casually behind her. As she set the glasses out on tables by the sauna, she became acutely aware that they were starting to undress. At first she thought that they were going to swim, but as she finished her task and picked up her tray to leave, she saw that there were a dozen men standing in a wide circle around her. Some of them were naked. Others dropped their pants as she looked up. She shot a glance from face to face, seeing the same expression on each one. They seemed to think that they could have her. One man already had a full erection. Someone said, 'Let's play chase the maid!'; the others responded, 'Yes!'

Glancing around for Max or Safronne, Jodi found they were not there. 'Oh no,' she croaked, putting up her hands. 'I'm not playing.'

A tall, dark man stepped forward and smiled reassuringly. 'But it's just a game. We wouldn't hurt you, Jodi.'

She shook her head. 'I said I'm not playing. Where's Max?'

They pretended to look around, but Max was not among them. The dark man took another step towards her. She could not back away for fear of coming close to those behind her. He came another step, his erection wagging at her, his balls swinging with each step. 'I'm sure if you join in the spirit of the game, you'll really enjoy yourself.'

Jodi glowered at him. 'Go to hell.'

'Look, we'll put the lights out to give you a sporting chance. But whoever catches you first has you to himself. We wouldn't be so unsporting as to gang up on you.'

Jodi shook her head. 'And I told you, I'm not playing your game. So kindly stand back – I want to pass.'

He smiled. 'But you have to play. If you run now with the lights on, you'll still be chased. If you stay, you might evade us in the dark; so – don't be a spoil-sport.'

'I said *no*. Don't you understand plain English?'

'All right,' the spokesman said with a shrug, 'if you really don't want to play, then you're free to go. We promise not to fuck you if you really don't want to play.' The circle nodded their heads, too seriously, she thought.

Jodi took her cue. She held her head up high and walked out through the circle.

She marched out through the changing room, but when she reached the door she found that it was locked. Turning sharply, she saw the group of naked men by the pool, their faces grinning widely.

As Jodi steeled herself, the lights went out plunging them all in blackness. She smiled grimly. She was not a novice at the hunt, and if she knew anything about wild creatures, it was how they hunted – or avoided being caught.

She reached up quickly and found a water pipe she'd noticed running through the room. Slipping out of the tight garment which would have handicapped her, she lunged for the pipe and swung. Quickly she moved along it until she reached a locker beside the door to the pool area, and she climbed on top of it. Her naked breasts hung loosely and her vulva was stretched as she crouched. Curiously, she was excited by the chase. Thinking about how aroused she'd been when Bentonne had hunted her, she slipped her hand between her legs to feel how hot she was there.

She could hear deep breathing as the first of her

pursuers came into the room, but she still couldn't see anything. A voice whispered into the darkness, 'Where are you, little pussy cat?'

'She's here somewhere, the little tease,' another answered. 'I'll spank her lovely arse when I catch her.'

'Don't you mean *fuck* her lovely arse?' As they laughed, Jodi held her breath, frightened they would hear her heartbeat. Voices receded into the gym and then returned.

Ten minutes must have passed, with a lot of swearing and shouts of 'Give up. We'll catch you soon'.

'Perhaps the minx has slipped back into the pool room,' someone suggested.

'Cunning little thing,' another hissed. 'Perhaps she's crept into the sauna.'

There was the sound of shuffling feet and all was quiet. Jodi stifled a sigh of relief: so far, so good. But what if they switched the lights back on and found her squatting naked on the locker? There was no way she could fight so many off. She doubted that they'd keep to their rule: first to catch her would have her for the night. She wondered what it might be like to be tied up and taken by so many men at once. For a moment, a tremor of excitement rippled through her. She quelled it and thrust away the thought. She would not give the bastards the satisfaction.

She froze as she heard a sound below her. Then there was the scrape of metal very close. Deep breathing just below her started coming close . . . Had someone thought of looking on the lockers?

A hand came out and caught her leg, but how the hell had he found her? 'Get off me,' she rasped, hitting out at the arm.

'Don't be afraid,' the owner of the hand hissed as he grabbed her ankle.

She kicked out and caught him on the shoulder. There was a stifled cry and the step ladder he had used went rattling across the floor.

Jodi caught her pipe and swung down, but her hunter grabbed at her leg and hung on tightly. As he pulled her to the floor and clasped her around the waist, she felt his erection hard between her legs.

She dug him in the ribs and made him grunt, but he widened her legs and thrust. She felt his penis slide and fill her but she wriggled on it and managed to get free.

By this time there was a hubbub in the pool room. Guessing where the doorway was, she made a dive, rolling through and to one side, just as several pairs of feet shuffled past. Now she tried to remember where the sauna was. But it would be silly to hide in there; she would be trapped if anyone came to search it. She racked her brains for the safest place to hide, then moved on her hands and knees in the direction of the pool. She bumped into a pool-side chair, and then stood and bumped into a man, her hand accidentally finding his half-hard penis.

'Don't do that, old chap,' he hissed at her in Dutch. 'I'm not gay. Go and find the girl.'

Jodi moved away without a word, breathing a sigh of relief. As she slipped into the water, she gasped for breath. Then she realised that if they put the lights on, she would be well and truly trapped. But if she hid behind the floating chair, they might not see her.

She groped about and found she'd reached the shallow end and rested, listening to the hubbub. Then an arm around her waist made her squeal out, but the hand around her mouth stifled it.

'What was that?' someone called. Footsteps came towards the pool.

'I stubbed my toe on a bloody chair,' her captor called

155

out in Dutch, holding Jodi tight around the mouth. Then he whispered in her ear, 'Don't be afraid. I'll get you out of here if you don't make a fuss.'

She nodded her head. She was getting cold and knew that sooner or later someone would catch her. But how had he found her? Was it the same fellow as had reached for her on top of the locker?

His body was warm against hers as he drew her to the steps and stopped. She could feel his penis against her bottom as he held her. As she floated in his clasp, his penis slipped into her again. She gulped and closed her legs, unwilling to cry out and bring the others. His lips came down on her shoulder and he kissed her tenderly, whispering, 'Do you promise not to try to escape if I let you climb the steps?'

She nodded again.

He withdrew himself from her and let her climb, then took her hand and guided her quickly; how, she did not know.

'Who's that?' a voice shouted close to them, as a hand reached out and touched her arm.

Her captor dragged her away, spitting into the darkness, 'It's me, you fool.'

'Sorry old chap, the voice retorted, 'I'm getting pissed off with this game. This vixen's too cunning tonight. What say we turn the lights on?'

'Yes, turn them on,' a chorus of voices called. 'She must be here somewhere. Then we'll toss for her.'

'Or play a hand of cards,' another called out. 'Winner take all.'

Jodi's captor steered her quickly from the men.

'Why don't we share her?' someone shouted.

'Yes, why not? She's led us a merry dance. Put the lights on!'

Now a chorus started. 'Put on the lights.'

'We'll take a vote.' Jodi recognised the voice of the dark spokesman. So he was not her captor.

'All in favour of putting the lights on and sharing her around, say yes.'

Her captor's chest against her back, she was pushed forward. There was the sound of a door opening and closing and a bolt being shot. Shit, where had he taken her?

Then a muffled cheer went up and a chink of light showed underneath the door. It was followed by shouts of 'Find the wretched girl'. At any moment they were sure to find her and her captor.

He held her so close she could feel his belly pumping, and his penis thrust against the crevice of her bottom again.

'She's not in the sauna,' a voice called out, so near that Jodi thought they'd been discovered.

'Then where the hell is she?'

'I don't know, for Christ's sake. Look for her yourself.'

Warm hands came up around Jodi's breasts. They held her gently so that she didn't feel molested.

'I don't know who you are, but don't think you can do what you like with me,' she snapped over her shoulder.

He kissed her shoulder again. 'Are you going to fight me then?'

'I will if I have to.'

'They'll hear you if you struggle. If they find us, I can't guarantee that they won't all want to play with you.'

She didn't recognise the voice, as the words sifted into her ear.

The door beside her rattled; she froze and the hand came up around her mouth again.

'What's in here?' a gruff voice asked.

'It's the control box for the pool heaters and the sauna, I think.' The door rattled again. 'Anyway, it's locked. I think we might as well give up. Go and tell the women they can come down now. At least we'll have some fun with them.'

All went quiet, but Jodi and her captor stayed stock still. Her captor's hand slid to her breast again and she dared not fight him off for fear of someone hearing. Minutes passed, while he pulled at her nipple very gently. It drove small tremors of energy down into her womb. She liked his touch.

'Who are you?' she whispered over her shoulder.

'A friend.'

'What's your name?'

'What do you want it to be?'

'I don't want it to be anything.'

'Then explore me and find a name that you think suits me.' He took her hand behind her back and made her close her fingers an his shaft.

'Go to hell,' she whispered, dragging her hand away despite herself. The feel of a strong, warm cock in her palm always turned her on.

He kissed her neck tenderly and fondled her breasts. To her annoyance she found herself moistening more. The touch of his warm flesh and the confines of the space made her body become more interested in him still.

'I said go to hell!' she hissed again as his hands slipped down her belly to her mons. 'I'm not doing anything with you.'

'Shall I throw you to the others, then?'

She shook her head violently. 'No, don't.'

'I won't if you're nice to me.'

'How nice?'

He laughed softly and drove his tongue into her ear. 'Teach me the best way to fuck a woman.'

She turned her head towards his mouth. 'You're doing pretty well already.'

'Thanks. It's the first time I've touched a real woman.'

'You're joking.'

'I've never been more serious. I've only fucked a few silly girls. You're so sophisticated compared with them.'

Now Jodi smiled resignedly. 'You're Hans, aren't you?'

'Correct,' he whispered sending his tongue into her ear.

'But I thought you'd left.'

He bit her neck. 'That was a ruse, my darling. But are you sorry it's me?'

'Why should I be sorry?'

'Because you think I'm only a boy?'

'Did I give you that impression?'

'Yes, you did . . .'

She turned to face him. 'Well, I don't think so now.'

'Honestly?'

'Why would I lie to you?'

'You might lie if you were trying to seduce me,' he laughed.

'I don't think you need much seducing. But why did you pretend to leave?

He laughed again. 'I had to make preparations for your capture.'

'What do you mean?'

'I had to make sure it was me who got you.'

'Did you know what they were planning, then?'

'Of course. We do this at every party, but I never get the girl. But tonight I had a plan. I wanted you like crazy and I didn't want anybody else pawing you.'

'That's very gallant of you.'

'Perhaps you wouldn't think so if you knew why I wanted it to be me.'

'Tell me – as if I couldn't guess.'

'So – I could finish what you started in the cellar before you tricked me.'

'And if I say you can't?'

'Then I'll let you go.'

'To be caught by the others.'

He kissed her neck and whispered, 'No. I'm not prepared to see you mauled by those bastards out there.'

She stroked his face and drew him towards herself. 'Thanks. I really appreciate that.' As her lips touched his, she felt him sigh. 'And thanks for rescuing me. But how did you manage to find me in the dark?'

He laughed softly again. 'I brought an infra-red night sight with me. It picks up body heat and enables one to see people in the dark. While all those fools were groping around, I spied you crouching naked on that cupboard.'

'And you brought me to some kind of control box?' She groped around and touched some dials and switches.

'Yes. It's at the back of the sauna. I put a bolt on the door in here as part of my plan.'

She kissed him again. 'Good boy.'

'So you do think I'm just a boy.'

'I'm sorry. I didn't mean it that way.'

'How did you mean it then?'

She kissed him lightly on the lips and held there, savouring the taste of champagne that lingered on them. 'I meant that you're very youthful. And I find you very attractive. My heart didn't stop thumping all the time I was stripping you in that cell.'

160

'And did your cunt go wet?'

She pushed him sharply. 'That's not the kind of question you ask a lady.'

He nuzzled against her neck. 'I'm sorry. You must find me very naïve.'

She kissed him long and tenderly. 'I find you very refreshing.'

'Good. So, *did* your cunt get wet as you bared my prick?' He laughed quietly and bit her ear.

'Yes, it did,' she whispered into his.

'And is it wet now?' He breathed into her mouth, his lips nearly touching hers.

She took his hand down to her mons, wound her fingers over his and made them curl into her furrow.

He didn't need more tuition than that. He slipped his hand deeper through her legs. Then, as he curled one finger up inside her, she opened her legs to give him better access.

Now he worked her slowly and very gently, as if he were exploring every bit of her. His touch was just as gentle as Safronne's touch had been. This man had not learned to be rough yet, and she liked it.

'You're very wet,' he whispered, slipping his finger up between her labia. 'Does that mean you want me to fuck you?'

'I'm not really sure.' she whispered teasingly.

'But if we don't, what shall we do? We might be in here for hours before the party finishes.'

'We could talk about the weather.' She slipped her hands over his smooth chest.

'I'd go mad if you did. I don't think I could stand being shut up with you for long without . . .'

She ran her finger over his lips. 'Without what?'

'Without doing something.'

'What kind of something?'

161

He kissed her passionately for some seconds. 'Whatever kind of something you want.'

She kissed him on the neck, then ran a line of kisses down his chest. His skin was silky smooth, and his chest hairless. As she reached his belly, it tightened. She felt the head of his penis underneath her chin as she set more kisses around his navel. Only when her mouth reached his pubis did she find a mat of curly hair.

Outside the cupboard, high-pitched laughs and screams told Jodi that the women had come down to join the party. She could imagine what was going on, but returned her attention to the young man's penis as she put her lips to it and kissed, from its root up to the glans. He sighed as she stretched her tongue and found the web, delighting in the feeling as she made the glans swell large. Now she ringed it with her lips, tracing the helmet form, settling her tongue into the groove and licking very slowly.

He moaned and thrust his hips out. 'It's the first time anyone's sucked my cock,' he whispered. 'But you'll make me shoot if you do that any more.'

So aroused that she could not stop herself, Jodi ignored his warning. His cock was long for one so young, but also very stiff. It curved up strongly as she pushed his foreskin with her lips.

'I'll come in your mouth if you're not careful,' he whispered. 'I'd rather shoot my spunk in you, but I haven't got a condom.'

'Bad planning,' she said naughtily. 'But I've got a coil.' He breathed deeply into her mouth again. 'Do you like it in your mouth?'

'Sometimes.' So fired up, she pushed her tongue between his lips and kissed him passionately, fencing with his tongue.

'Fucking hell,' he whispered. 'You've got me so hard

it hurts. I think I'm going to come.'

She snaked her tongue into his ear. 'I'm sorry. Would you rather I stopped?' She smiled to herself, playing with him. It was delightful to have such a virile yet naïve young man at her fingertips. It was far better than tying Bentonne to the bed to have her way with him. And the danger of the situation was adding to her tension. They might still be discovered, but what the hell . . .

The sound of deep-pitched moaning on the other side of the door, and the words 'Fuck me. Fuck me harder!', accompanied by the unmistakable rhythmic grunts of coitus, only served to raise the tension in the cupboard.

Hans and Jodi explored each other's bodies for some minutes, becoming more and more aroused. Deliberately spinning out the foreplay, Jodi worked them both to an explosive tension from which she knew she would orgasm easily, and possibly several times. She guessed he would ejaculate as soon as he entered her, and she was determined not to be left unfulfilled.

'Can I fuck you now?' he whispered.

'Don't be impatient.' She forced him to bend and put his face between her breasts. He took one in each hand and folded them about his cheeks, working the nipples slowly with his thumbs. Then he sucked each one in turn and returned his mouth to hers. It made her flush between the legs, and her nubbin yearned to feel the rubbing of his cock. She spread her moisture about her vulval lips, ensuring that she was slick for him to enter. She was so keyed up, she wanted it fast and furious.

Screams of ecstasy followed gasps of great relief on the other side of the door; then came clapping and loud cheers. Hell, there was an orgy taking place outside as well as inside that cupboard.

Hans bit her neck, rubbing his scrotum up and down her mons, and gasping, 'I've got to shag you now. If I don't, I'll shoot my jism up your belly.'

She didn't say a word but grasped his penis and slipped it between her legs. The sensation of it there made her tremble wildly. He bent his knees and pushed up hard.

Sighing as she felt his cockshaft slip through her nectar and his sweat, she clasped him around the neck and pressed her mouth to his.

As he lifted her under the buttocks, she curled her legs around his hips. Holding her tightly, he took her with great urgency, pushing her against the door. Each thrust made her rise on his hips, her clitoris grinding the root of his cock. 'Oh God,' she groaned, 'that's marvellous.'

'So are you,' he gasped. 'Your cunt's so tight I'm going to come. Oh, god!'

'There is someone in there,' a voice called out.

Jodi tried to make her lover stop, but he was lost in the sensations of the act and would not be deterred.'

The door rattled. 'It's locked from the inside,' a voice called out. 'Get a lever.'

Jodi beat at her lover's back. She tried to pull away but he pinned her to the door and drove up into her with such verve she found it was impossible to stop him. But did she want him to stop?

The banging at the door was matched by the banging of her back against it. Then it gave way.

With her legs wound round the Dutch boy's hips, they tumbled out to be caught by eager hands. But he had become so voracious for his climax he did not stop.

Jodi glanced up to find a ring of faces looking down with great surprise. Everyone was naked, the women looking haughty, the men with wicked grins. Hans continued to thrust between Jodi's legs, gripping her buttocks tightly. A loud cheer went around the throng and they all began to clap and chant, 'Fuck her. Fuck her, fuck her, fuck her!' to the tempo of the clapping.

Hans came with a triumphant cry as he drove himself in deeply. As Jodi felt him flush, her body came to a height of tension she had rarely felt before. Her muscles clamped as she felt him beat, and she sensed the fluid warmth as he filled her with his semen.

He gasped out 'Yes!' as he rose up on his hands and bent his back, and drove his penis in one last time as deeply as he could.

Jodi's climax came with such great force that the faces swam above her as glorious waves of hot sensation rushed up from her pussy to her breasts. Then they rushed back down again, swamping her, making her nipples tingle and her pussy's lips distend.

Another cheer went up. 'Well done, lad,' someone said as they patted him on the buttocks. Then they pulled him to his feet, his penis beating strongly. As Jodi looked up, it spurted once again, the warm fluid landing between her breasts.

Hans stood tall. He placed a foot on Jodi's shaven pubis and raised one arm in a triumphal salute.

As her body racked, she plucked her nipples and pulled her legs back hard.

He covered her pulsing pussy with his sole and worked her gently with his heel until she stopped her writhing. Then he tugged her up, gripped her around the neck and pulled her mouth to his. A louder cheer went up as he took her lips with passion.

She could not catch her breath. Then the passion turned to delicate little kisses on her lips, and biting motions down her neck – and all the while the group looked on and cheered.

Jodi didn't object. She'd had a momentous release, and she didn't care a fig about Van de Rohe's fancy friends knowing that she'd had it.

Now Hans sank to his knees. He took her nipples one by one and sucked. She stood with her legs apart, her head held high, and her cheeks afire with energy.

The circle murmured as he knelt and put his lips against her mons And when he sat between her legs and took her pussy in his mouth, the murmurs turned to gasps.

Jodi spread her feet and closed her eyes.

He ran his tongue between her secret lips. He took her nubbin in his mouth and pulled. Hell, the thought of being watched so closely, and the sensations he was eliciting aroused her need to come again.

As her clitoris rose, she frogged her legs and spread her crevice for his mouth. Now she rode him, pushing out her hips and leaning back. She put her hands about his head and pulled him hard into her crotch, willing him to fuck her with his tongue.

He bit her playfully in the groin, then rose slowly up her body, setting little love bites on her flesh. He reached her breasts and pulled her teats between his lips, then took her mouth again.

Jodi felt quite frenzied. He'd worked her up once more and left her unreleased. Now it was she who sank down on her knees. A cheer went up as she took his cock and plunged it into her mouth. Conscious of the watching eyes which seemed to stoke her passion, she grasped the youthful shaft and sucked it hard.

He worked his hips and fucked her mouth, pulling her on to himself just as Bentonne had done in front of that blazing fire. But to hell with Bentonne – this was happening now . . .

Without warning, Hans broke away. He let out a

whoop of triumph as he swung Jodi off her feet. Cradling her strongly, he pushed through the spectators and ran into the pool. In the shallows he beached her, lying on top of her, warming her with his body. Slipping his cock into her, lifting her buttocks from the tiles, he drove a finger deep into her anus. Then he fucked her hard and fast, his eyes ablaze with success as she wracked on him and gasped to every thrust.

Buoyant in the water, she was able to move and twist and squeeze to get the best sensations from his cock.

He took her in a frenzy before he knelt beside her hips and raked her with his semen. As it spurted in the air, a cheer went up around the pool. Quickly, Jodi took his cock and aimed it at her mouth. Then they floated for some time, with the whole of him inside her, and kissed and hugged and floated in their bliss.

They were celebrities that night. Everyone looked on her with awe. The men could not do enough to make her feel most welcome, and the women even smiled.

The party had gained momentum now. Jodi and Hans sat back and watched as couples mated in the pool. On her hands and knees, Maria Hagen had one cock in her mouth; another filled her anus while she straddled a third man who licked her pussy.

Jodi became quite tense again as Hans had not brought her off a second time. She needed him badly now. Her spirits sank when he rose and kissed her tenderly.

'I really do have to go now, Jodi. I'd love to fuck you all night, but I have to get back to my university for an exam at eight. I'm sorry.'

She held him tight and closed her eyes until he drew away.

'Do you forgive me for kidnapping you?'

She stroked his cheek and kissed his nose. 'What – from the forest, or tonight?'

He held her close and smoothed her bottom with one hand. 'Both times.'

'I suppose so.'

'Good. Can we meet again?'

She looked him in the eyes. 'I don't know. I shan't be here for long.'

After Hans had left, the party seemed quite flat. Safronne did a striptease, doing hand-stands and gambolling, her legs spread wide to show her quim. Then two men held her up and stretched her out while a queue of men stood between her legs, rubbing themselves off until her body was covered with their cum. All the time she wriggled and giggled, massaging the thick fluid over herself to make her skin shine richly.

Jodi became progressively more charged and needed a release, but didn't want any other man but Hans that night – not even Max who still had not come down.

Jodi went sadly up to Safronne's room, her body still alive.

Standing before the mirror she stripped her garment off, turning in the moonlight to watch it light her swollen breasts. Then she caught a movement from the bed.

'Hello Jodi,' a soft voice said. 'I wondered when you would come.'

Chapter Thirteen

JODI COULD JUST make out the form of Anna, Countess Dehousen, sitting in Safronne's bed. She had her cloak about her, but her breasts showed through the folds.

Jodi backed away but came against the door.

The countess stood and floated in the gloom towards her, her hands outstretched.

'Get out of here,' Jodi snapped. 'This is a private room.'

'For private assignations?' Anna whispered as her fingers locked with Jodi's and she drew her to the bed.

'No,' Jodi croaked. 'I don't want you.'

'But I want you, Jodi, my dear. I need you.' The blue eyes shone.

'Go and find someone else.'

Anna shook her head. 'There is no one but you for me tonight.' Her strong hands held Jodi and made her sit.

Jodi shook, not so much with fear as with awe. The clear eyes searched her face for compliance, the gaze electric, setting up currents in Jodi's belly.

'I need you,' Anna whispered. 'And I think that you need me.'

'Why should I need you?'

'Because I know a secret, my dear.'

Jodi froze. What could this woman know that involved her?

Anna held her fingers tightly and moved up close. 'Please me and I'll tell you. You will thank me all your life.'

Jodi closed her eyes for a second. 'Does it involve Max?'

Anna simply smiled demurely.

Jodi looked into her eyes far some moments before she asked, 'What do you expect me to do before you'll tell me this dreadful secret?'

'Fuck me.' Anna said it with a look af excited expectation and Jodi felt that she'd been hooked.

'I beg your pardon.'

Anna gazed into her eyes. 'Fuck me hard, and I'll tell you what I know.'

Jodi closed her own eyes and concentrated. The woman was clearly drawing her with her secret. It might just be a ruse to get her compliance in some erotic act. But could she ignore it? She thrust the thought away.

Her expression must have shown that she was puzzled. Anna ran a hand around her face, then trailed her fingers down Jodi's breast, pushing the nipple upwards.

'Please don't,' Jodi whispered.

'But you like it! See how your nipples rise?'

'I can't help that. Please go.'

'But if I go, you will not learn something important about yourself.'

'I know everything there is to know, thank you.'

'Do you, my dear?'

'Yes – I do.'

'Very well. Let us see. Now – why don't we talk

about the way Max's cousin fucked you in that cottage?'

Jodi looked at her hard. 'How did you know about that?'

Anna smiled. 'I have seen the pictures, Jodi.'

Jodi glowered. She'd give Max a piece of her mind in the morning.

'Wasn't he magnificent, darling?' Anna whispered as she stroked Jodi's hair. 'I wish a man would treat me like that.'

Jodi felt her eyes go wide. 'But he was a pig. He treated me appallingly!' It was not entirely true, but she would not excuse Bentonne's behaviour.

'Exactly, my dear. Quite appallingly.'

Jodi held her breath as Anna stroked her nipple. She recalled Hans having said something about this woman being a masochist. But what exactly did that mean? She had the feeling she'd soon find out.

As Anna slipped away her cloak, Jodi saw that she was naked. Her heart began to pound. Still keyed up from her wild night at the party, she stared.

The countess was magnificent. Her breasts were large but firm, the nipples very brown against the pale, soft skin. Her waist was trim, her belly flat and her neck had swan-like grace.

Anna's touch was loving and, as she stroked, Jodi found her annoyance began to wane. She could have got up and left, but something held her there. Was it the allure of the beautiful woman, or the promise of a secret? She didn't really know, and as Anna took her hand and kissed her fingers one by one, she began not to care.

Jodi's hand wandered up to Anna's breast; her fingers stroked the smooth, elastic flesh and wandered to the nipple. She ran a finger round the nimbus, feeling the ring of little pimples as they rose to meet her touch.

171

When she traced Anna's wide, full mouth, she had an urge to kiss it. They sat and touched each other for some time, and Jodi became more and more aroused.

'I saw you fuck that boy,' Anna said wistfully as she lay back in the pillows, her breasts hanging heavily.

'I rather think it was the other way around,' Jodi whispered.

Anna put out a hand and touched her arm. 'Did he hurt you?'

Jodi shook her head. 'No. He was very strong and quite unstoppable, but he didn't really hurt me.'

Anna smiled wistfully again. 'They never hurt me. Perhaps they think I'll break.'

Jodi raised an eyebrow. Anna held her gaze and said nonchalantly, 'And they never last long enough to make me satisfied.'

Jodi mouthed an 'Oh', and put her head back. She could relate to that! Most men didn't take her hard enough or long enough to give her total satisfaction.

Anna stroked between Jodi's legs and leaned close to her as she whispered, 'I need it very hard, Jodi. I need a brute.'

Jodi put her hand on one warm thigh. 'I know how that feels.' She was beginning to feel some empathy with the woman. That strange excitement which had run between Safronne and herself was running now with Anna. This woman had her alight with curiosity, if not raw need.

Anna drew Jodi gently to herself and kissed her cheek. Jodi did not resist when Anna offered up a nipple to her mouth. She took it, and as Anna held her to her breast she feit a curious mixture of calm and excitement.

Anna thrust the breast out harder. 'Would you beat me, Jodi?'

Jodi raised her head from the nipple.

'Would you beat me and tell me what a slut I am?'

'But you're not a slut; you're beautiful.'

Anna laughed softly. 'That is just my front, my dear. Inside I'm just a slut. And sluts should be punished, don't you agree?'

Jodi took the nipple again and sucked it slowly. Bentonne had called her a wonderful slut and then taken her hard on that plane. Was it some kind of power game men played? And did the countess need to be subservient to that? She thrust the thoughts aside. This was no time for fathoming such things.

'So will you thrash me and then fuck me hard?'

Jodi looked up again. 'I don't understand how I could.'

As Anna delved beneath the duvet, Jodi stared. The slender, well-manicured hand brought out a flail with little leather thongs at the end of a whippy shaft. And then she pulled a dildo out, a double-shafted rubber cock, and pushed it into Jodi's hand. Jodi's eyes went wide as it looked so real, even though much larger than a normal cock would be. It felt so firm to touch but was softly covered in a supple skin. The foreskin rolled just like the real foreskin of a man. When Jodi accidentally felt the testes, a surge of thick, white fluid welled up from each glans.

Her hands trembled as she held it.

Anna fixed Jodi's eyes and whispered, 'Strap it on. See how it feels to be a man. Dominate me like any man has dominated you. Feel how Bentonne felt as you cowered under him by that tree.

Jodi threw her head back righteously. 'Bentonne was a brute.'

'Then experience how it feels to be a brute. Show me the anger you felt towards him when he hit you. Whip me, and pretend you are whipping him. Dominate me until I beg you for release, just as you begged him. Call me a slut, a tart, a cunt. Beat me until I cry out for you to fuck me.'

Jodi could not stop shaking as Anna made her kneel and pushed one shaft of the dildo deep between her legs. It filled her fully, the testes hanging against her thighs. Then Anna took some ointment and smeared it on the shaft until the rubber shone.

Jodi now stood between the woman's legs as she lay back on the bed, holding the whip in one hand and tugging the foreskin of the cock with the other. Each tug moved the other shaft inside her. It made her feel so horny. In the dressing mirror at the bedside she looked for all the world like a rampant man; apart from her full, round breasts glowing in the moonlight. This and the sight of the woman under her, with her legs pulled back made Jodi quiver with excitement.

'Scold me,' Anna whispered. 'Tell me what a slut I am, strike me with the flail and call me a fucking whore.'

As Jodi looked down on the countess, sternness rose inside her and she pushed her pelvis out to thrust the cock. She began to feel so strong and overbearing as she straddled Anna's shapely legs.

'Now . . .' she growled in imitation of the bass tones of a male, but couldn't stop herself from smiling slightly, 'now – I'm going to punish you. Open your legs, you slut!'

Participating excitedly in the game, Anna squirmed while Jodi whisked a toe between her legs. Anna wriggled on it, trying to make it penetrate her.

'You whore,' Jodi growled, moving her toe. 'Have you no shame?'

Anna shook her head, and worked herself on the toe. As Jodi raised the flail and struck across her shoulders, Anna arched her back. It was not hard enough to hurt – just enough to make her sting and bring her flesh to life. Curiously, it made Jodi's vaginal muscles tighten, too. She struck again with little, stinging lashes, catching the swells of Anna's breasts and the hollows of her flanks. She turned and stood facing Anna's feet, her own feet beside Anna's breasts. Then she laid the whiplash gently between her stretched-back legs. And all the time her tension rose within her until she was a mass of pent-up energy.

The leather caught the tightened flesh by Anna's secret lips and made them spasm with the sting.

Now Jodi stroked the flail over Anna's inner thighs and the triangle of her pubis. The tip of the thongs just wrapped around her mons, fell inside her furrow. Jodi could see her clitoris stand proudly.

She whipped Anna's belly and her flanks, each stroke getting harder as her energy surged. Her breasts were tight, her nipples hard, and the nectar from her pussy flowedy hotly down her leg.

Jodi turned again, putting one foot on Anna's belly; pressing down she felt omnipotent. She thrust the cock out proudly. She threw her head right back as she struck again, growling, 'Do you repent, you harlot?'

'No, 'Anna sighed, 'I don't repent. I need to be admonished with that brute of a cock of yours.'

Shaking uncontrollably, Jodi sank upon her knees, pushing Anna's legs back. In the mirror at the side Jodi saw the huge and shining phallus poised above the woman. She looked down between the straining legs, and saw what any man would see as he prepared to thrust. And she also felt what any woman feels when she has a fully rampant cock inside her.

The rubber shaft felt huge between Jodi's legs as it forced the woman wide. Jodi pushed and then withdrew, flexing her hips just as a man would do. But when she buttressed her arms beside Anna's, her breasts hung down. It was strange to have a woman's breasts swinging above her captor while the organ of the male thrust in deep between her legs.

'Feel my cock, you harlot,' Jodi croaked, getting into her role now. 'Pull your legs back further, and squeeze me with your cunt.' She grimaced to herself: that was what men had said to her, and it always turned her on.

Anna squeezed the phallus, subservient to Jodi. She seemed not to feel it as a threat but to enjoy the hugeness of the thing deep inside her body.

Then her eyes lit up as Jodi began to fuck with greater force.

'I'll fuck you, you tramp, I'll fuck you,' Jodi growled over and over again, the power of her position driving her deep into the role she had taken on. She had begun to vent her anger at some man. All men? At Bentonne, in particular.

'Oh, that's so good!' Anna cried as she wriggled on the dildo and thrashed her head from side to side. 'But I need it harder. Whip me!'

Jodi withdrew and glared down at her conquest. The ample breasts were rolling as Anna thrust her hips. Her nipples stuck out strongly, her belly rose and fell. Then she turned and knelt and thrust her bottom out at Jodi. She set her head down in the pillow and pushed out a huge and swollen pussy.

Jodi closed her eyes, breathing in her scent – and then she struck at Anna's bottom. The flail came down on the rounded forms, making Anna jolt. But a cry of pleasure witnessed that the countess liked the lash.

As Jodi lashed again and then again, white weals appeared on the soft, smooth skin, then slowly turned to pink. Jodi had the impulse to cast the flail away and use her hand instead.

The first slap stung her palm; the next shot a bolt of energy right through her. Anna cried out, 'Yes!

Jodi spanked, her fingers just touching Anna's secret lips, slick from sheer excitement. At the end of each spanking stroke, Jodi paused, her fingers resting just inside those lips, feeling their slickness, their heat and steady pulse.

As Jodi spanked again, the phallus jogged, making the one inside her jolt as well, and giving her an urge to thrust it in.

She moved again and aimed it, pressing the glans against Anna's pouting lips as she parted them with her thumbs. Then she spanked Anna's bottom hard and filled her with the cock.

Anna began to cried out loudly. 'Harder. Oh – that's nice.'

Now Jodi was lost in the sensations rushing through her. She had never felt such trembling excitement. As she watched the phallus sink up to its hilt, she pressed her pubis to the cushions of her conquest's bottom; so warm and soft against her thighs.

Now Anna began to push back on the cock, driving its counterpart deeply into Jodi. She rammed herself against its balls to make its fluid well.

Jodi raked her slender back with one hand while she pulled her own nipple with the other, arching her spine and throwing back her head.

Now she lost her head and she began to fuck so hard and fast it took her breath away. Her breasts bounced fully to each thrust, as the cock inside her drove her to a frenzy. She spanked and thrust, hissing, 'Slut. You wonderful slut,' just as Bentonne had done to her. And as she spanked and thrust again, she recalled what her ex had done to her – the bastard – but she'd loved it.

They both climaxed together. As Jodi drove the phallus in, Anna let out a shriek and began to judder. The whole of Jodi's body went into rigours of contractions. Her belly cramped, her vaginal muscles tightened, then released. The rubber cock inside her seemed to fill her more than any man's had ever done, and as she pressed it deeply, she felt its fluid spill.

Jodi rested on Anna's back; both of them gasped for breath. She fondled Anna's breasts while Anna's body pulsed against her own. Then Jodi laid her on her back and pushed her legs back gently, exposing the heaving woman to her gaze. She put her mouth to her soft, hot flesh and kissed; the scent was musky and sweet at once, and it sent tremors of excitement to her crotch again. The texture of the labia was smooth to her lips as she dragged her tongue tip through them.

When Anna's rigours ceased, she turned over and put her head between Jodi's legs, taking Jodi's clitoris and sucking on it, while Jodi put her head back and pushed her pussy down on to the tongue. Together they licked and probed and kissed until their tension rose once more.

Unable to restrain herself, Jodi pushed the woman on her back and forced her legs apart until her pussy gaped. Then she bowed her back and thrust the cock between its swollen lips, driving it both to Anna's extremities and her own. Bracing herself on her hands, she fucked her powerfully but slow, her breasts swinging to every push, her clitoris chafing on Anna's mount. Then as Anna's climax came, she arched her back, letting out her tension in a scream that started in her belly and ripped up through her throat.

In sympathy, Jodi's own vagina went into spasms so terrific that she gasped with every one. They heaved together in small paroxysms of delight, each moaning as the other shuddered. As Jodi collapsed on Anna, their nipples rode and slid in their sweat. Jodi's vulva cramped and loosened with repeated orgasmic pulses for some time. Then, when they quietened down to little trembles of pleasure, they lay head to toe, their faces buried between each other's legs, and sucked their pussies lovingly until they fell asleep.

Chapter Fourteen

WHEN JODI WOKE, Anna had gone. Had their liaison been a dream?

She shook her head, sloughed the duvet off and lay naked, looking up at her body reflected in the mirror. Then she stretched and opened her legs so she could see her furrow, still moist from the encounter. Slipping her finger through it she smiled and thought of Anna, and the way the woman had lain in wait, determined to have her way with her. How different that experience had been to those with Bentonne or Max, or even Hans. How much more fulfilling . . .

She thought about Max, and wondered if he might be cross with her for letting Hans have her in that cupboard. But had he been there, the whole event might not have happened, so perhaps she should be cross with him for that. He would be flying off to London for that Board meeting, so she would have to catch him before he left. Then when the business with Bentonne was out of the way and the man had been sent packing, she and Max could perhaps settle down to some kind of normality. She was in no hurry to leave the house, since Max had become more than fond of her and she of him.

She was headed for the shower when she caught sight of a note on the dressing table addressed to her. With trembling hands, she unfolded it to reveal large, flowing writing:

Hello, Jodi, my love,

   Thank you for fulfilling my wildest dreams so wonderfully. Perhaps we may meet again sometime.

   Love, Anna

P.S. Here is the little secret I promised you. I observed that you sometimes show a streak of anger in your manner when talking to men. You might be happiest if you assert yourself more strongly over them just as you dominated me. Screw them, darling, just as they have screwed you.

'How dare she,' Jodi hissed as she tore up the note. 'Who the hell does she think she is – some headshrinker?'

After Jodi had showered, she dressed in a pair of Safronne's jeans and a tight pink T-shirt. Her breasts bounced heavily as she skipped down the stairs. But her joy was cut short as she bumped into Polders coming from the direction of the pool. He carried a diving mask and a black rubber wet suit dripping with water. Glowering at her, he pushed her aside and passed on.

After a leisurely breakfast Jodi went in search of Max. She wanted to speak to him sternly about the way he had shown the pictures to Anna, but she was conscious of feeling guilty for making love to Hans and Anna instead of keeping herself for Max.

Since things had worked out so well, she hummed to herself as she strolled along the corridor. She hadn't felt happier or so free for a long time. Perhaps Anna had been right after all. By allowing herself to express that anger that she had held down for so long, she had rid herself of the tension it had brought.

She hummed again, as she neared Max's study door. But she stopped as it opened and she heard Polders's voice. Determined to assert herself as Anna had said she should, she prepared to stride in breezily, when Polders spoke again.

'And the girl, sir. What shall I do with her?'

'After you've had your fun with her, get rid of her too,' Van de Rohe said coolly.

'But sir – I thought you were fond of her.'

Van de Rohe laughed. 'She was amusing for a while, that's all. And she was a fine attraction for the party and useful for Hans to practise on. Did he give you my night sight back, by the way?'

'Yes, sir. It was a good idea of yours, to give that to Hans.'

Van de Rohe laughed. 'Thank you, Polders. He deserved it as his bonus for doing such a good job with the photos my cousin Maria Hagen asked us to get. She's always had fantasies about Dean and paid me a fortune for the pictures. Substituting herself for the Barens girl, she's going to have them blown up to life size, so she can paper her bedroom with them and pretend he's fucking her while she frigs herself off.'

Polders's guffaw made Jodi shudder.

'Now – remember to take those spare fuel pods from the plane and that damaged wing we replaced last month. Dump them with Bentonne and the girl in the sea far enough out to be certain they don't swim to shore. Then I'll put out a press release about the plane crash.'

'Very good, sir. Will that be all, sir?'

'Have you finished transferring the last gold shipment?'

'No, sir. The last is still at the airfield. We haven't got any more room for it here. I had difficulty this morning getting the grille to shut. Apart from that, the police have been snooping around the airfield and we thought it wise to leave it in the tanks for now.'

'All right. But don't leave it too long. Someone might just have the bright idea of searching them. This will have to be the last consignment until I am established as controller of Bentonne Universal.' He laughed. 'I have much work to do before I catch my flight to London.'

Jodi was fixed to the spot, totally shocked by the realisation that the Dutchman had fooled her completely. And he *had* been smuggling gold.

As Polders came out and crashed into Jodi, she pulled her wits together. Polders glared and caught her by the arm; dragging her painfully back into the study.

'Look what I found skulking outside the door,' he said to Van de Rohe in Dutch.

Van de Rohe stared at Jodi for a moment, then smiled as he addressed her in Dutch as well. 'Good morning, my sweet. How are you? Have you recovered from your riotous night?'

Jodi's mind whirled. She was about to reply in Dutch when her sense of self-preservation stopped her. She looked at him blankly, then managed a thin smile. 'Don't speak your gibberish to me, Max dear. You know I don't understand a word of it. What was it you wanted to say?'

Van de Rohe smiled and kissed her cheek. 'I was just inquiring how you were, my sweet.' Then as an aside to Polders in Dutch, 'Don't worry, man, she doesn't suspect a thing. Be ready to take me to the airport in an hour.'

Polders threw Jodi a dark look and left. Van de Rohe took her in his arms. She almost vomited as he kissed

183

her forehead, and nearly kneed him in the groin but stopped herself in time.

Looking up at him, she managed a sweet smile.

He kissed her tenderly on the nose, then eased her away. 'I must finish some work before I leave for London. You go and amuse yourself, but don't get up to mischief.'

She pouted girlishly. 'When can we make love again?'

He ran his fingers over one breast and toyed with the nipple through her T-shirt. 'I'll be back later tonight. Shall I take you to the gym and tie you to a vaulting horse while I spank you?' He laughed. Then he whispered in her ear, 'Or shall I fuck you in the sauna like I did before?' She pouted again as he ran a finger up between her legs. 'And stay away from my cousin while I am away. You know he's very dangerous.'

Yes, Jodi thought. Bentonne must be very dangerous to you if you're planning to have him disappear.

She put her lips to his and kissed him lightly, wanting all the time to take him by the balls. But she contained her anger and sidled sexily to the door, blowing him a kiss as she said, 'See you later, lover.' I'll see you in hell, you bastard, she thought as she closed the door.

Jodi went quickly to the kitchen, pleased that Safronne was not there. She found a serrated knife and bounded up the stairs to the attics, already hot in the morning sun. She was surprised to find Bentonne lying on the bed with only one wrist tied to the frame. Covered in his blanket, he looked up angrily.

'You slut,' he growled, then glanced at a portable TV set. 'You cheap little slut.'

She stopped and stared at him. Then she stared at the television. Her eyes opened wide as she saw herself and

184

Van de Rohe on the screen. They were both naked in the sauna, Van de Rohe standing over her, his cock rearing. The bastard must have had a camera in there.

When the scene moved on through that sweaty encounter, Bentonne glowered as he watched Van de Rohe stroke her breasts. On screen, she made a pretence of escaping, but he caught her by the shoulders and pushed her down. She wriggled again to no avail, his hands slipping to her breasts, her nipples poking out between his fingers. But then she wound her legs around his hips and tried to pull him down.

Jodi's mouth dropped open as she watched the TV. She saw the tip of Van de Rohe's shaft as it nudged momentarily at her pussy. Then he thrust it and she watched her image smile widely and close its eyes as it sank between her legs.

When she looked at Bentonne, his face was white with anger. 'I didn't know,' she stuttered. 'I didn't know there was a camera in there.'

'Two cameras, actually,' he sneered. 'But would it have made any difference if you had known about them? Don't you get a buzz out of watching and being watched?'

The screen went blank for a moment, then to Jodi's surprise, the film started again. She looked at Bentonne with a query in her eyes.

'The bastard's got it on a loop,' he sneered. 'It's his way of letting me know he's taken you away from me – and that you enjoyed it.

Jodi snapped the TV off, but her hands would not stop shaking and she dropped the knife. Bentonne looked at it cynically as she picked it up. 'Now you've taunted me with that film, I suppose you've come to slit my throat.'

She marched to the bed angrily, holding the knife

above him. 'Don't tempt me, Bentonne. I must say it wouldn't take much to make me do it.'

'Then why don't you? You've got what you wanted, haven't you? No doubt he's paid you handsomely as well as giving you a few good fuckings.'

She struck him hard across the face. 'You're an uncouth bastard, Bentonne. Now apologise, or I swear I'll doctor you right here.' She ripped the blanket off him and grabbed him by the testes, holding up the knife as she did so.

Bentonne paled. 'All right. I'm sorry. I didn't really mean that. I was angry about that video.' She relented and let him go, although it had given her a buzz to hold him by the balls again.

'OK. But one more crack out of you and I'll leave you behind.'

His eyes lit up and he sat up quickly as she sawed at his bonds, conscious all the time of his nakedness.

'My god, you're beautiful when you're angry, Jodi. Do you know that?'

She clipped him about the head. 'Shut up, you. Give me any more of that slop and I will leave you to your fate.'

'What fate? Having that Indonesian nympho playing with me again?'

'You'd be so lucky! No. Your precious cousin plans to have us dropped in the sea tonight. He's faking a plane crash.'

'He wouldn't be so stupid.'

'Do you want to bet? He's got a lot to lose. Your hunch about him smuggling gold was right.'

Bentonne's eyes studied her with admiration as she savagely sawed the plastic bonds, distracted at the sight of his penis wagging to every movement.

'But how did you find out?'

She threw her head back. 'By applied intelligence. I'm not as stupid as you seem to think.'

'I've never said you were stupid. Get me out of here and I'll show you how much I value you, Jodi.'

'Value me? Like some hired tart, do you mean?'

'I didn't mean it that way.'

'Yes you did. People like you always gauge something by what they have to pay for it.'

'My god, you've become bitter.'

'You bet I have. Now, for Christ's sake shut up while I cut this through.'

The wrist strap gave way at last, and Bentonne sprang up. Jodi threw him his blanket and marched to the door. Then she heard footsteps in the passage.

'Quickly! Back on the bed—' She pushed him back. 'And pretend your wrist is still tied.'

He did as he was told as she slipped quickly underneath the bed.

The sight of Polders's feet in the open doorway made her freeze. She'd been a fool to leave the door open.

'Where is she?' the Dutchman growled.

'Where's who?'

'Don't play games with me, mister.' There was a sharp crack, like the flat of a hand on a cheek. Then all hell was let loose as Bentonne sprang and tackled Polders to the floor.

Jodi slid out from under the bed and side-slipped to the door, narrowly missing being flattened by the fighting men. Polders threw himself on Bentonne and pinned him by the throat.

Bentonne twisted and got on top.

Jodi watched with fascination as his testes bulged through his legs while he struggled with the Dutchman. Among a tangle of arms and legs, Bentonne's half-hard penis pushed against Polders's thigh, and his face went

187

purple as the Dutchman's huge hands took his throat to cut off his air.

Jodi shook herself, ran back into the room and picked up the portable TV. She crashed it down on Polders's head; he groaned and slumped on Bentonne. Frantically she pulled Bentonne's arm, dragging him from under the dead weight of the moron.

She slammed the door, and a wave of sickness welled up inside her. Her hands trembled so wildly that she could hardly hold the bolt to shoot it to. She took control of herself and towed the gasping Bentonne along the passage. They reached the top of the stairs only to be met by footsteps coming up – and Van de Rohe's voice.

'Polders? Polders, where the hell are you? I'll miss my flight, you cheese-head.'

When there was no answer, the footsteps resumed. Jodi pulled Bentonne back along the passage to the room with the loading door. She dragged him in and shut it quietly, putting her back to it as he gasped for breath.

A few minutes passed before they heard a shout. 'Well, they didn't pass me.'

'Then they must still be up here, sir.'

'Then find them, you dolt. I'll wring that minx's neck when I get hold of her.'

Jodi gestured to Bentonne to move a crate, but it was too heavy to lift and the scraping brought the two men immediately, just as Bentonne slammed it hard against the door.

'You can't escape,' Van de Rohe shouted. 'Give up and I promise I won't hurt the girl.'

'Go to hell!' Jodi shouted back as she took up a coil of rope and flung the loading doors wide. Leaning out perilously, she reeled at the sight of the busy street, the green water of a canal glinting in the sunlight. She managed to slip the rope over the pulley on the gantry. Then she looped a free end through the necks of several heavy sacks. When she looked around, Bentonne had his back against the door, the muscles of his torso and his thighs straining as he pushed. His penis curved up strongly. She thrust aside a mental query about how a man under threat could get aroused, pushed the sacks over the edge, and watched the rope snake past her. A shout from below and the loud screech of brakes followed by the sound of breaking glass told her it had landed.

'Come on!' she screamed at Bentonne. 'Leave that and grab this rope.'

He looked at her and then at the rope. 'But who's going to work the winch?'

'No one,' she grinned, adrenaline coursing through her system. 'We're going down together.'

'But that's madness. We'll be killed.'

She gave him a look of desperation. 'Staying here won't improve your health too much either. But stay if you're too chicken to risk it.'

She grabbed the rope, and he took hold of it above her head. Just as the room door burst open, they launched themselves into space.

The counterbalancing sacks nearly knocked Jodi off the rope as they passed on their way up. Their weight was less than the combined weight of herself and Bentonne, and they accelerated alarmingly fast.

They hit the ground and rolled, to a gasp from a small band of incredulous onlookers standing around two crashed cars.

Letting go of the rope, Jodi struggled to her feet. Then someone shouted, 'Look out!' and pulled her aside just before the sacks hit the ground and spilt their contents of coffee beans over the cobbled roadway.

The siren of a police car sounded close by. Then mayhem ensued, with people jabbering at Jodi while others pointed at Bentonne, standing naked and confused, his phallus rearing stiffly.

Chapter Fifteen

DRESSED IN A clean pair of jeans and a white wool sweater of her own over a pink blouse, Jodi stood in the doorway of a large, old-fashioned kitchen. Her Aunt Maria busied herself with laying the table for lunch. She greeted Jodi as if she were a child who knew she had committed a misdemeanour.

'Your uncle has called Jan de Vries,' the old woman said cheerfully. 'He's something big in customs now. I'm sure he'll be able to help you. But Uncle is very cross with you, Jodice. He didn't expect that his favourite niece would behave as you have. Fancy prancing in the street with a naked man – and in the state he was in, too.'

Jodi managed a contrite look. 'I'm sorry, *Tante*. And thanks for paying our bail. If you and Uncle Maarten hadn't come to rescue us, I don't know how long we might have been in jail.'

The aunt scowled at Dean Bentonne as he arrived in the kitchen, looking clean and bright. A crisp white shirt turned up at the collar did not quite hide a red weal from a rope burn.

They lunched in silence since Jodi was still not prepared to be over-friendly with Dean Bentonne. But she was glad she had helped him escape from Van de

Rohe. Now, all they had to do was wait for her old friend, Jan de Vries. She hoped that he would be able to induce the local police to start an investigation of Van de Rohe's premises. After all, kidnapping was a serious offence, not to mention smuggling gold. She'd managed to keep her mouth shut about the gold. It had been better to get out of police custody first before launching an investigation.

De Vries arrived after half an hour of awkward silence. Jodi gave him a peck on the cheek as she pulled him down into the chair beside her. Then he looked at Jodi with the kind of intensity only an experienced interrogator of miscreants can muster.

She told her story as matter-of-factly as she could, although she missed out the details about the sexual encounters.

'Firstly,' De Vries said seriously, fixing Jodi's eyes with his, 'how do we prove that Van de Rohe kidnapped you? He might say you were making up the story.'

Jodi threw her head back haughtily. 'I can prove he had us flown here in the luggage compartment of the plane if you can locate it.'

'And how do we identify the plane? There are several in Van de Rohe's hangars. We have been keeping a close eye on them for some time.'

Bentonne sat up, frowning. 'Do you two mind not talking in double Dutch? I can't follow a thing.'

De Vries nodded slightly. 'We have been investigating your company for some time, Mr Bentonne.'

Bentonne sagged noticeably.

De Vries seemed not to care. 'But so far we have not had any grounds for forcing a search of Van de Rohe's promises. Now Jodi, how can we prove your story of being kidnapped?'

'Look in the luggage compartment of the plane – one registered in England, I think. Three of the registration letters are GWF. I didn't catch the first letter.'

'And what should we expect to find?'

Jodi grinned widely. 'Under the rubber matting you'll find a gold ring engraved JMB. It's the ring you gave me for my twenty-first birthday, Jan.' She pecked him on the cheek and looked at him with a grin.

De Vries scowled. Then, as he looked at her with admiration, Jodi felt a flush of pride. 'You always were a clever girl, Jodi. All right, if the ring is there it might indicate that you put it there at some time. But how do you prove when that was? And more importantly, how can you prove that Van de Rohe has been smuggling gold? It's your word against his that you overheard him talking about it.'

She smiled again, pleased that Bentonne, too, was looking at her with new respect. 'Look in the spare fuel tanks of the plane. The one in that van they put us in had something heavy in it that clunked when I kicked it.'

The afternoon dragged. It was stifling hot again and Jodi lay on the bed in the room she always had when she stayed with her aunt and uncle in Amsterdam. It was her second home. With her personal things and a wardrobe of her clothes, she thought that she might stay on for a while and not go back to England.

In the next room she could hear Bentonne bumping about and tried not to imagine what he was doing as she stripped to take a shower and cool off. But just as she had turned on the flow there was a soft knock at the door.

She shut the water off and called, 'Who's there?'

'It's Dean. Can I speak with you?'

'Go away, Bentonne. I don't want to talk to you.'

'But Jodi, at least let me apologise to you.'

She snatched up a bath towel and wrapped it around herself. Then she opened the door cautiously but did not let him in. 'All right. Apologise.'

Dressed in a silk dressing gown of her uncle's, he was drying his hair with a towel. 'I need to talk with you seriously.' He looked around the landing as if someone might overhear. 'Won't you let me in?'

'Say what you have to say and go. Jan should be back at any time, so make it quick.'

'You're a hard woman, Jodi,' he sighed.

'No harder than men like you have made me, Bentonne.'

'I'm sorry.'

'What for? For seeing me have a good time with your cousin?'

'Don't be cynical. It doesn't suit you. I'm sorry you were treated in that way. Maximillian has always been madly jealous of me when it comes to women. Showing me that video was his way of getting even with me for taking his girl when we were younger.'

'I'm not interested in your childish squabbles with your cousin. Now apologise for the way *you* treated me, and then go.'

'But I thought you liked the way we made love at the cottage.'

She felt a flush of annoyance at that assumption. 'I hated every minute of it. I think you're a conceited, boorish prig. And as far as our making love is concerned, I think you're a wimp. I found your cousin far better than you as a lover.'

Anger rose to his face as he pushed the door. She tried to keep him out but he was too strong for her. The towel dropped away as she fell back on the carpet. He

194

was astride her in a second, looking down on her nakedness. Glancing between her legs, he smiled.

Confronting him at the door, the sense of being in control and being able to tell him to go to hell had aroused her. Or had it been looking into those dark brown eyes again? Her body had responded just as it had under that tree in the forest, and when he had sat on the end of her bathtub.

'Get out of here,' she gasped, winded from the fall. She tried to rise but he pushed her down with his bare foot. Placing it on her belly, he held her firmly.

'I'll go when I've said my piece, Jodi.'

'I'm not listening to your excuses.' She struggled against the pressure of his foot, but it only stimulated her more. Powerful and dominant, he stood above her with his arms on his hips and his eyes fixed on hers. The dressing gown bulged at the crotch, his penis hardly hidden behind its folds. Her breasts lolled from side to side as she tried again to wriggle free.

He grimaced. 'Lie still. I'm not letting you up until you listen to what I have to say.'

'And I'm not listening to any more of your excuses.' She squirmed and slipped sideways, sprang up and faced him angrily, her fingers outstretched to claw him.

He grabbed at one hand and twisted, pulling her towards himself.

She tried to escape his grip, but he was too strong. She kicked out at his crotch; he sidestepped and grinned. It seemed that he was enjoying a tussle with her again.

'You think you're very clever, don't you?' She hit him across the face with her free hand. 'But I've got news for you, mister. Just because you're rich doesn't mean that you're any cleverer than I am.' She kicked out wildly and caught him on the shin.

'Stop it, you little hell cat,' he barked as he pushed her on to the bed and threw himself on top of her to stop her flying arms.

She felt his hardness against her mons. Then his knee came up between her legs and he pressed her shoulders down into the pillow. She looked up at his face, his breath combatting hers. Then his mouth came down.

She struggled to get him off her, but with his knee ground into her crotch, she was becoming more and more aroused. His mouth worked hers strongly, and she liked it.

The kiss turned more loving as she quietened. The knee between her legs began to massage slowly. His dressing gown spread open and she could feel herself wet against the warmness of his knee. She could also feel the hardness of his penis as it rubbed against her thigh.

'Hell, you're beautiful, Jodi,' he whispered as he kissed her nose. 'And so clever.'

She turned her face away with pretended annoyance. 'And you're a pig. Get off me before I scream rape.' She closed her eyes as a tear ran down her cheek.

He sat up and looked down on her. 'I'm sorry.'

'For getting me into this mess?'

'No, for holding you down like that.'

Jodi wasn't sorry about that. In fact she wanted the brute more than ever. But he had got her into a hell of a mess and until she was completely clear of it, she would not give him the slightest hint that she was still attracted to him for some reason she couldn't fathom.

As he ran his fingers between her breasts and into her navel, she pushed them away and sat up, only to find his penis jutted out between the folds of the dressing gown.

Jodi shook her head. 'Christ, you're a horny brute. Put it away.'

He smiled. 'Is that what you really want?'

'Yes, it is.' She cast her eyes down and away, her pulse speeding at the sight.

He slipped his fingers between her legs and stroked her moistened labia. 'You're a rotten liar, Jodi.'

'I can't help what my body does. My mind says that you're trouble, and for once I'm going to do what it says.'

He reached forward and kissed her again.

She pushed him away, but he took her hand and wrapped her fingers around his cock, making her work his foreskin. He clearly knew that this would make her soften her hardness towards him. The man was a devil, and she hated him. But she loved him too, in a strange kind of way . . .

When the doorbell rang far down in the hall, a wave of disappointment ran through Jodi. 'I expect that's Jan,' she said, as she peeled her fingers away from his shaft. 'Now put this monster away and let me get dressed.'

Bentonne sat on the bed and watched as she dressed. Bracing himself on his arms, his penis jutted unashamedly. When she stepped into a pair of skimpy panties, she almost felt his eyes on her mons. She dragged the sheer material over the stubble of her hairs, not caring what he thought about her being shaved. She stretched her pink T-shirt above her head; her breasts hung tautly and bulged nicely as she wriggled it on. Then she bent over Bentonne, touched the web of his shaft lightly with one finger to make it pulse, and wrapped it in his gown. 'Put it away, I said. I'm not going to play your game anymore. Now, are you coming down to see Jan de Vries or not?'

'What's news, Jan?' Jodi asked. She stood in the kitchen with Bentonne close behind her. 'Did my tips pay off?'

The Dutchman pulled a small transparent packet from his pocket. Inside it was a golden ring.

Bentonne smiled at Jodi.

De Vries maintained an inscrutable face, but his eyes danced animatedly. 'We found your ring under the rubber matting as you said. And when we examined the auxiliary fuel tanks, we found traces of gold in them.'

Jodi nodded wisely. 'They were working the old silver egg routine.' Then she folded her arms and looked at the men, keeping them in suspense.

De Vries gave her a good-natured frown. 'Come on Jodi, we men aren't as clever as you. And we aren't mind readers either.'

She smiled demurely. 'Well, in large uninhabited areas like the South African veldt, pilots of small planes use wing fuel tanks for added range and safety. My native friends in more northern parts used to tell stories of great birds which landed, dropped their silver eggs and then flew away with new ones under their wings.'

Bentonne gave her a puzzled look.

She tossed her head triumphantly. 'When I began to fly with my father, I realised that some pilots were changing wing tanks. Instead of just filling the ones that were attached to the aircraft, they would remove one empty pair and put up a pair of filled ones. But it didn't make sense to me at the time.'

She could see by the frowns that it didn't make sense to the others either. De Vries sat pan-faced, but his eyes betrayed his interest.

Jodi felt exhilarated.

Aunt Maria appeared with coffee and macaroon biscuits, while Jan prompted Jodi impatiently, 'Go on. What was the logic behind the changing of tanks?'

'I think those aircraft were used for smuggling diamonds and gold across borders, and the wing tanks were packed with their illegal shipments. Of course the tanks contain fuel as well. Flying low over the tree tops, they touch down in some remote place where the auxiliary tanks are swapped. Then they take off again within minutes. Another plane comes in, picks up the original tanks with their illicit cargo, now refilled with fuel, and flies another leg up country. In this way the secret payload is relayed across vast areas. The clever thing is that each aircraft stays in its own area where it is known and so doesn't arouse suspicion.'

De Vries was nodding approvingly. 'Good. I hope you're right. I've raised a warrant to search Van de Rohe's premises. I want you both to come with me. We'll see what he has to say about smuggling gold and kidnapping you.'

'But that's preposterous, *Mijnheer*.' Maximillian Van de Rohe sat back behind his desk and stared coolly at De Vries. Jodi wandered around the room casually picking up ornaments, while Bentonne stood at the side of the desk and scowled at his cousin. A burly policeman took up the doorway.

Van de Rohe looked at De Vries smugly. 'Your men have searched the house and have not found anything incriminating, and yet you persist with your ridiculous claims of smuggled gold. And as far as kidnapping my cousin and Miss Barens is concerned, that's quite bizarre. You have found no bed in the attic or the cellar. You have no proof that he or anyone else was imprisoned there. My cousin brought Miss Barens as his fancy piece when he came here to a party last night – that's all. Any story Miss Barens has spun you about her being here for several days is a lie. And as for my cousin . . .' He scowled at Bentonne. 'Dean has always been a troublemaker. He has stayed in this house before. I'm sure he can describe it minutely. The truth is that I found him in the attic this morning with his clothes off and Miss Barens over a sack as he spanked her. When they found they'd been discovered, they performed that crazy stunt out of the loading door.'

Jodi snorted. 'You won't get anything more than lies from him, Jan. Let's go and find Safronne. She'll tell the truth.'

They trooped to Safronne's room and knocked. When her almond face appeared at the door, she looked surprised.

'Who are these people?' she asked Van de Rohe in Dutch as he pushed the door open. Completely naked and shining with little beads of water from the shower, she seemed entirely unabashed.

'This is *Mijnheer* De Vries from Customs,' Van de Rohe said lightly. 'He is investigating some silly rumours about us and these two people. I told him that—'

De Vries stepped forward smartly showing his warrant. 'They say they were here for a few days, miss. Do you recall them at all?'

Safronne looked from Jodi to Bentonne, and shook her head.

Jodi was shocked. She reached out to touch her arm. 'But Safronne! We slept together. We made love, Please don't lie.'

Safronne studied her coldly. 'I'm afraid I don't recall seeing you.'

Jodi was angry now. 'Then how do I know that you have a prominent mole inside your leg?' She pushed the girl back on the bed and forced her legs apart. When she stretched the skin between Safronne's pussy and her thigh, a large mole was clear to see. As she glanced at De Vries and Bentonne, Jodi couldn't care a damn about their embarrassment as they looked between the girl's long legs.

Safronne looked quickly at Van de Rohe, then back at De Vries as he flung her a robe. 'Ah – I do recall this girl at the party. Forgive me; I have a very bad memory for faces. She must have seen my mole when I performed a striptease to amuse the guests.'

Jodi stared down at her derisively, but the hard look in the dark eyes told her that it was no use persisting with Safronne. The girl was clearly scared.

Jodi turned to De Vries and spoke in Dutch. 'I was here for three days; until this morning when we escaped.' She glanced at Van de Rohe to see that his face was white and continued in her best Dutch. 'You might have thought that I was ideal for your dirty job, but my agent seems to have neglected to tell you that I am fluent in your language. I heard you this morning talking to Polders about the gold and about getting rid of us.'

She turned to De Vries. 'And I've just recalled that Polders mentioned something about a grille. I saw him coming from the pool room with a mask and wet suit this morning and thought it a bit strange. There's a grille at the bottom of the pool, and I wouldn't mind betting they've stashed the gold down there.'

Van de Rohe's face drained as De Vries gave sharp orders, then looked at Jodi. 'What other surprises have you got for us, miss? You still haven't proved your story completely.'

She grinned and knelt by Safronne's bed. Pulling out the newspaper she had stashed there, she showed the date. 'I put this paper under the springs on the day I arrived here. Do you see this thumb print?' She flashed the paper around. 'If you have it analysed, Jan, you'll find that it's mine. And if you examine the vent in the

201

storeroom we were kept in, you'll find my initials and the date scrawled in the dust. I doubt that they will have cleaned that out.'

Bentonne looked blank. Jodi guessed that he had not understood a word, but she could not stop to explain.

De Vries rubbed his chin and asked in English, 'Why would you hide things wherever you went, Jodi?'

'To prove I was there at that time, of course. That's why I left the ring under the rubber mat in the plane.'

She turned to Bentonne. 'And if you look under the bed in your cottage, Mr Bentonne, you'll find a small handkerchief with an embroidered rose stuffed between the floorboards.'

Bentonne raised an eyebrow. 'But why?'

She threw her hair back triumphantly. 'In the bush, when the native people travel, they often leave a marker at certain spots. It tells other travellers they have been there, and when. I've kept that habit over the years. And when I found myself in this mess, I realised that it might be important later.' She grinned at the assembled faces and walked casually from the room.

Chapter Sixteen

JODI STOOD IN the forest clearing with her pulses beating hard. Strong afternoon sun heated her breasts through her blouse, but a storm was brewing in the distance.

The game-keeper's cottage looked asleep, with its shutters closed across the windows, the chimney giving out no smoke.

In the pocket of her jeans, Jodi nervously fingered a large door key and took a deep breath.

At the porch she inserted the key and let the door creak open. Was it only four weeks since she had first heard that sound as Dean Bentonne had carried her dripping over the threshold? It was already three weeks since she had arrived back in England. It had been three weeks of evading Bentonne's phone calls and his letters; except the last one, which had contained the key.

Everything inside the cottage was positioned as Jodi recalled it, but the room was cold and lifeless. Her memories held more warmth and excitement than this reality.

Her briefcase and her camera bag sat on the kitchen table; the cavernous bathtub was empty, the fire in the black range out.

She took a handwritten note from the pocket of her jeans and read it for the umpteenth time – she could not recall how many.

My dearest Jodi,
I was so sad that you would not speak to me on the phone. You were out on two occasions when I called at your flat, so I'm writing in the hope that you will read this letter and respond. Just ring my secretary. She will find me and I will come to you from anywhere in the world.

I'm desolate without you. Life seems not to have much point now; even as Chief Exec. of Bentonne Universal, I find my world is empty.

Cousin Max is awaiting trial on smuggling charges. Polders turned against him and spilled the beans. I shall be abroad for a while, starting to put your ideas into practise.

Your papers and camera equipment are safe in the cottage for you to collect whenever you like. I enclose the key.

I love you.
Dean

Tears coursed down Jodi's face as she picked up her things. Head down, she went slowly into the other room. At the bed, she set the bag down, bent and pulled a small handkerchief from a crack between the floor boards. Spreading it out, she laid it on the pillow.

A beam of sunlight from the open doorway lit the handkerchief like a spotlight. She wiped her tears with the back of her hand.

Then the spotlight went out. The sun had been extinguished.

She turned.

In the doorway a tall man stood, silhouetted against the yellow light of a stormy sky. For a moment Jodi froze. She knew the profile, but she could not see the expression on his face. Was he angry? Was he sad?

As her eyes became accustomed to the glare, she saw that he stood half naked, stripped to the waist, his torso glistening with perspiration; a simple woodcutter or game-keeper? He slicked back his hair with one hand and planted both fists on his hips, his legs splayed widely.

As Jodi focused, the features of his face emerged from the shadow, his dark eyes showing sadness. His firm mouth did not bend into that smile she'd liked so much.

Her breasts heaved under the cotton blouse as she breathed heavily, her nipples thrusting through the thin material as if demanding his attention.

'I lied about being abroad,' he said softly, and smiled with uncertainty.

They both stared. For Jodi, time seemed to stand still. Then she gathered her senses. 'I wondered why you sent the key, you scheming . . .'

His forehead creased in a frown. 'I didn't know any other way of getting you to myself. I need to talk.'

She threw her head back. 'There's nothing to say. The whole affair's over.' Then she frowned at her choice of words but shrugged it off.

'Is it over, Jodi?'

'Yes, it is.'

'But what about my offer of a position in the company?'

He had sent her a contract which she had thrown into the wastepaper basket, but it had not got as far as the dustbin yet.

'I don't want your job, thank you.'

'But you would be in charge of improving conditions

for our Third World workers. Isn't that what you wanted?'

Yes, it was, but not if it meant being subservient to him. 'I'll think about it, OK?' She brushed her hair back and shouldered her bag. 'Now please get out of my way. I have to get back to London.'

He caught her arm. 'Stay for a while.'

'I don't think that's a good idea.'

'That depends on whether or not you want to finish what we started.'

'What *you* started, you mean.'

He shrugged. 'OK. What I started.' He seemed not to want to argue but his closeness and his scent was getting to her again. Her body was coming alive to him just as it had in the bedroom at her aunt's.

He took her camera bag and set it on the bed. Then he picked up the handkerchief and put it to his lips.

She flicked a hair back from her forehead. 'I didn't think you were the sentimental type, Bentonne.'

'I wasn't until I met you, Miss Barens.'

The thunder storm growled in the distance. 'Oh god,' she sighed half aloud, 'I'll get soaked again if I don't hurry.'

'So you'd better stay until it's passed.' His eyes showed hope.

'I'll only stay on condition that you keep your hands to yourself.' Jodi stood her ground, her hands on her hips as he came close.

He put up his hands in surrender, but kissed her on the forehead.

'And you can stop that too.'

'Is that what you really want?'

She scowled. 'Yes it is. It really is, this time.'

'So the fact that your nipples are rising doesn't mean that you're aroused?'

'Just leave my nipples out of this, will you?'

He smiled. 'OK. I won't mention them again. But why are your jeans wet down there?' He nodded to her crotch.

Jodi was aware that she was damp. No matter what she had decided to do as far as this man was concerned, her body always seemed to have other ideas when he was close to her.

'A girl can get moist without wanting to screw, you know.'

He raised an eyebrow. 'All right. If you say so.'

'I do. Now, why don't you go and make some tea. I'm parched. I'm going out to get some air before that storm breaks.' The truth was that she couldn't stay with him for long without feeling really horny. Part of her said she must leave; another part demanded she stay.

She strolled out to the place where she had hidden with her camera. The lake shone in the storm light, little ruffles whipped up on its surface by a rising breeze. It seemed so long since she had watched Dean Bentonne on that shore.

Jodi sat in the grass with her back to a sticky pine tree. Her inner conflict worried at her as she stared at the gathering blackness in the sky. Then her attention was drawn to the cottage door as Bentonne appeared, stripped of all his clothes.

'Damn him,' she swore aloud. 'What's the fellow up to now?'

He seemed not to notice her. Running to the pool, he dived straight in, swimming strongly for some minutes. Then he hauled himself powerfully out and stood dripping on the landing stage.

When he set his legs apart and bent to touch the grass, she whispered, 'Oh my god,' and wished she'd brought her camera.

After he had bent and stretched, he turned, the pelt of his pubis coppery in the yellow light. As Jodi tried to focus, she could see he was aroused. It was not a full erection, but enough for his cock to stand out from his thighs.

The inner surfaces of her own thighs trembled and her stomach churned. When he raised his arms above his head, thrust out his hips and closed his eyes, Jodi was trying to work out some logic for his performance. Then as he looked up and peered in her direction, she suddenly understood. As he moved towards her, she had to think fast. If she refused to play his game he might get mad at her. She had always quaked before him when he had been angry and had succumbed to his will.

Her heart began to skip beats as he loped across the clearing. Her mouth went dry, and a charge began to build between her legs.

She took off through the forest, not caring when branches caught her summer blouse and ripped it. It flapped about her shoulders as she fled, her breasts bouncing freely, her hair flowing out behind her. This time she was not soaking wet from the storm and she ran easily and fast – this time she might evade him. But did she want to? Wasn't this what she had fantasised about?

Behind her, muffled steps were plain to her heightened hearing even above the harshness of her breathing. Now she burst into the clearing with the oak tree at its centre and decided to make her stand against him there. She snatched up a whippy fir branch and set her legs apart.

Dean Bentonne stopped. He stood, unabashed, his legs splayed widely, his head held up and his phallus erupted just as proudly as it had before. This was definitely not what she had planned when she'd come to get her gear.

It took only a few heartbeats for him to reach her in long strides. Now he stood before her, grinning.

'I suppose you think this is clever,' she gasped, and tried to avoid looking at his erection but could not. It rose before her as her eyes travelled up his panting torso to his dark-brown eyes. She fixed her gaze on his, trying to determine when he would make his move on her.

The wide mouth broke in a knowing smile and his eyes locked on to hers. 'Isn't this what you came back for, Jodi?'

'No, it isn't. Now get out of my way. I'm going to get my gear and leave.'

He grabbed her arm strongly. 'No you don't, baby. If nothing else, you're going to stay and talk about the job.'

'There's nothing to talk about.' She pulled her arm away from his hand. 'I'm not interested in your display or your job.' Liar, she said in her head. The man was turning her to jelly again. But she kept her eyes homed in on his, aware that her own eyes were alight.

As she faced him squarely, pale sunlight broke grey sky, highlighting the undulating muscles and his youthful features. All he had to do was stand eyeing her, and her resolve melted by the minute.

As he moved towards her, Jodi backed against the tree. 'Don't think I'm going to fall into your arms again, Bentonne.'

He simply smiled and moved in on her.

'You're a cocky bastard,' she whispered as his mouth touched hers.

'And you are the most tantalising woman I have ever met, Miss Barens,' he whispered.

Her legs went weak as Bentonne, silent but intense,

yoked her neck. With her eyes level with his mouth, she stared, fascinated by the full lips as they pursed. Hotter now, his breath forced itself between her lips and made her pant with raw excitement.

As his lips closed on her mouth, her fingers touched his skin, felt his muscles rippling. Then her palm slipped down and stroked his penis.

He took a long breath and let out a little sound of pleasure. 'I knew you wanted to play.'

'You assume too much,' she whispered as he continued to kiss her lightly.

'And which fantasy do you want me to play out for you?' The kiss was cool and sweet and Jodi felt her excitement rising. Then he pulled away just far enough to break the contact with her lips. 'Well? Which is it to be?' He undid her buttons and peeled away her blouse. Then he slipped her zip and stripped her jeans, leaving her in just her skimpy panties. Kneeling to put his nose to her crotch, he drew deeply of her scent, then drew her panties down.

She let him remove her shoes and clothes to leave her naked.

He widened her legs, and as she felt his tongue draw deeply through her furrow she whispered through a smile, 'You're a bastard, Bentonne, and I hate you.'

He set little kisses up her belly to her breasts, and his shaft came up between her legs, pressing on her mount.

She moved to feel his hardness better. Her throat released an involuntary little moan as his lips traversed her cheek and whispered into her ear, so softly she could hardly hear the words. 'I think you just want fucking.' He thrust his tongue into her ear and pressed himself against her.

She groaned, feeling the warmth of his chest against her breasts, and then she took his lips by storm. As he withdrew to set a line of bites down her shoulder she cried out, 'Oh my god!' with every one. Molten with her need, she wriggled herself against his cock, almost delirious to feel its length inside her.

He pulled her to himself, his penis thrusting upward, stretching her secret lips, then drove a finger deep into her anus.

She let out a shriek with the pleasure-pain that gave.

'So ... what fantasy do you want, Jodi?' he whispered. 'How do you want to be fucked?'

'Like this,' she hissed, biting him hard on the neck as she ringed his balls and drew him into the clearing. She made him lie down in the grass, and pushed back his knees to spread them widely.

As she stood over him with the fir branch in one fist, the impending storm rumbled overhead. She set about his legs, his belly and his chest, making him flinch to every stinging lash. But he grinned as he tried to fend her off.

She pushed him down and straddled him, and thrashed his belly hard, the fronds at the end of the branch bringing colour to his skin. Then she rose and pulled his cock right up, spread her legs and sank on it. Then she growled as she flayed his arms, 'Now fuck me, you randy bastard. Fuck me until I come. And don't you dare shoot or I swear I'll flay you within an inch of your life. Show me how much better than your cousin you are.'

That did it.

He thrust up with such force that her breasts bounced almost painfully, but the feelings between her legs were so marvellous she didn't care a damn.

She closed herself tightly as he thrust, making him force himself into her, opening her out, spreading her widely until his pubis met her clitoris.

When a flash of lightning lit the sky she thrashed him with the branch and rode him like bucking bronco.

Then the storm broke with a crash.

Jodi came in a crescendo of contractions, each one clamping so hard she wondered if it would stop.

He raised his hips and drove his cock up through her yawning pussy as far as it would go, while rain streamed down her face and ran between her breasts.

Jodi felt a fluid warmth between her legs as her nectar mingled with the rain running through the crevice of her bottom.

Another wave of contractions came, making Bentonne moan; but he seemed to have managed not to climax.

Jodi began to laugh as her muscles gripped his cock and her tremors rippled through her. All the anger and the frustration of the intervening days seemed to wash away.

She rested with her hands beside his chest and looked down with elation, whispering, 'That was the nicest fucking I've had since Max screwed me in that sauna.'

Anger crossed his face, and she laughed aloud again.

He tried kiss her, but she rose. Standing over him, she placed the sole of one foot on his cock and pressed it to his belly.

He looked up at her with excitement in his eyes. 'My god, Jodi, where have you been all my life?'

She shrugged and turned away.

'Where are you going?'

She blew him a kiss. 'I'm going back to London.'

He sat up abruptly. 'But you can't leave me now.'

She smiled. 'Why not?'

'Because I need you.'

'You just need someone to screw whenever you feel

randy – and that's most of the time.' She pushed him down on his back and stood astride his torso, one foot on each of his arms, pinning him to the grass. She knew that he could see her pussy, wet with rain and her juices as he stared up, shaking his head with disbelief.

'No, you're wrong, Jodi I love you. I want to marry you.'

She raised an eyebrow. 'But do *I* want to marry *you*? Why would I want to do that?'

'Because I think you love me too.'

'Do I?' She smiled with elation.

'You don't have to say yes right now.'

'That's very considerate of you.'

'Come and work with me. Then you can decide if you want to marry me or not.'

As she stepped back and looked down on him, his shaft erupted more strongly still. She felt pleased that he had held himself back for her. Energy coursed through her as she knelt between his feet and pushed his legs back. Then she took his shaft in her mouth, making him buck and pant as she sucked it, pushing down his scrotum to tense the foreskin tightly.

He raised his hips and began to fuck her mouth, his eyes closed, his belly heaving. She clawed his belly with her nails, then drove a finger deep into his anus. He began to writhe on it and gasp; his cock went ridged, his balls drew up tightly and his belly hardened.

She thrust the finger hard.

Now he cried out and began to wrack on her finger, his cock becoming huge in her mouth. She tasted the saltiness of his pre-ejaculate as she drove her tongue against the web of the glans.

Her free hand raked his belly. Then she jabbed a finger between his navel and his cock, just as Safronne had done.

'Christ, Jodi,' he gasped, 'you're a witch. I'm coming . . . I'm coming! His body began to judder as he lay back on the grass. Keeping her finger deep inside his rectum, she withdrew her mouth. He arched his back and thrust his cock upward in fresh air.

'Don't stop now, sweetheart,' he gasped. 'For Christ's sake, don't stop!'

She thrust her finger and twisted again, watching his cock fuck air. Awed by its size, its thickness and pulsing length, her pussy began to weep. She widened her knees, pushing his legs farther apart, stretching his inner membranes. His testicles bounced as he urged to come, while her finger drove deeper until it was engulfed.

He began to moan, tears running down his cheeks. The skin of his torso was tight, beaded with rain. The helmet of his cock looked slick with her saliva and a bead of pre-cum which welled in the eye and trickled down the groove.

As she worked her finger through his anal ring, her thumb dug into his scrotum and pushed. Now the whole of his cock was tightly stretched, the veins pumping rapidly as he twisted and turned. But still he didn't come in the fresh air of the evening. She knew that he needed his dick to be engulfed, either by her mouth, her vagina or a hand.

Jodi sat back, spreading her pussy, long stems of grass tickling at its lips, and recalled Anna's note. She smiled.

Screw them, darling, just as they have screwed you.

She screwed him, jabbing her fingers into the smooth tunnel of his rectum, and the soft, elastic skin of his sac, making his balls stand out, heavy against her fingers.

Then her second climax came.

She put her head back and started to laugh, her belly

214

pumping and her breasts so tight they hurt. The lips of her pussy were swollen and hot as she rubbed them in the coolness of the grass. Juddering under the onslaught of the orgasm, which racked her, Jodi felt her finger in his anus vibrating too.

Still shaking as shooting darts of energising heat rushed from her open pussy to her breasts, Jodi took Dean Bentonne's hand and curled it round his cock. He threw his head from side to side. He raised his hips and arched his back as she made him work his foreskin with a steady motion, screwing it up tightly before she plunged it down.

Jodi waited until his masturbating strokes shortened, became harder and more rapid. Now he was skinning and wringing his penis, driving the head of it through his fingers as she squeezed her own around them to put more pressure there.

'I'm coming. Oh god, Jodi, you wonderful slut, I want it in your cunt!'

'But my cunt is not available at the moment, Mr Bentonne.'

He moaned and strummed his cock faster as she withdrew her fingers.

'Please, darling. Please, fuck me!'

Jodi leaned over him to kiss his gasping mouth and whispered, 'I said no, darling. Now – I'm going back to London. You lie here and play with yourself, and perhaps I'll call you sometime.'

Overexposed

THE X LIBRIS READERS SURVEY

We hope you will take a moment to fill out this questionnaire and tell us more about what you want to read – and how we can provide it!

1. About you ...

A) Male   Female

B) Under 21   41–50
    21–30   51–60
    31–40   Over 60

C) Occupation_____

D) Annual household income:
    under £10,000   £31–40,000
    £11–20,000   £41–50,000
    £21–30,000   Over £50,000

E) At what age did you leave full-time education?

    16 or younger   20 or older
    17–19   still in education

2. About X Libris ...

A) How did you acquire this book?

    I bought it myself
    I borrowed/found it
    Someone else bought it for me

B) How did you find out about X Libris books?

    In a shop
    In a magazine
    Other_____

C) Please tick any statements you agree with:

    I would feel more comfortable about buying X Libris books if the covers were less explicit

    I wish the covers of X Libris books were more explicit

    I think X Libris covers are just right

    If you could design your own X Libris cover, how would it look?

D) Do you read X Libris books in public places (for example, on trains, at bus stops, etc.)?

    Yes   No

216

3. About this book . . .
A) Do you think this book has:

Too much sex?
Not enough?
It's about right?

B) Do you think the writing in this book is:

Too unreal/escapist?
Too everyday?
About right?

C) Do you find the story in this book:

Too complicated?
Too boring/simple?
About right?

D) How many X Libris books have you read?

If you have a favourite X Libris book, what is its title?

Why do you like it so much?

4. Your ideal X Libris book . . .
A) Using a scale from 1 (lowest) to 5 (highest), please rate the following
   possible settings for an X Libris book:

Roman/Medieval/Barbarian
Elizabethan/Renaissance/Restoration
Victorian/Edwardian
The Jazz Age (1920s & 30s)
Present day
Future
Other

B) Using the same scale of 1 to 5, please rate the following sexual
   possibilities for an X Libris book:

Submissive male/dominant female
Submissive female/dominant male
Lesbian sex
Gay male sex
Bondage/fetishism
Romantic love
Experimental sex (for example, anal/watersports/sex toys)
Group sex

C) Using the same scale of 1 to 5, please rate the following writing styles you
   might find in an X Libris book:

Realistic, down to earth, a true-to-life situation
Fantasy, escapist, but just possible
Completely unreal, out of bounds, dreamlike

D) From whose viewpoint would you prefer your ideal X Libris book to be written?

Main male characters
Main female characters
Both

E) What would your ideal X Libris heroine be like?

Dominant	Shy
Extroverted	Glamorous
Independent	Bisexual
Adventurous	Naïve
Intellectual	Kinky
Professional	Introverted
Successful	Ordinary
Other	

F) What would your ideal X Libris hero be like?

Caring	Athletic
Cruel	Sophisticated
Debonair	Retiring
Naïve	Outdoors type
Intellectual	Rugged
Professional	Kinky
Romantic	Hunky
Successful	Effeminate
Ordinary	Executive type
Sexually dominant	Sexually submissive
Other	

G) Is there one particular setting or subject matter that your ideal X Libris book would contain?

H) Please feel free to tell us about anything else you like/dislike about X Libris if we haven't asked you.

Thank you for taking the time to tell us what you think about X Libris. Please tear this questionnaire out of the book now and post it back to us:

X Libris
Brettenham House
Lancaster Place
London WC2E 7EN